Warren Lee Goss

The Soldier'sThe Soldier's Story of his Captivity at Andersonville,

Belle Isle, and Other Rebel Prisons

Warren Lee Goss

The Soldier'sThe Soldier's Story of his Captivity at Andersonville, Belle Isle, and Other Rebel Prisons

ISBN/EAN: 9783744729253

Printed in Europe, USA, Canada, Australia, Japan

Cover: Foto ©Andreas Hilbeck / pixelio.de

More available books at **www.hansebooks.com**

THE

SOLDIER'S STORY

OF HIS

Captivity at Andersonville, Belle Isle,

AND OTHER REBEL PRISONS.

By WARREN LEE GOSS,

OF THE SECOND MASSACHUSETTS REGIMENT OF HEAVY ARTILLERY.

Illustrated by Thomas Nast.

BOSTON:

LEE AND SHEPARD.

1867.

8844
22/11/90

STEREOTYPED AT THE
BOSTON STEREOTYPE FOUNDRY,
No. 4 Spring Lane.

PREFACE.

———◦◦⋛⋌⋚◦◦———

IF the cause for which so many sacrifices were made — which so many died in prison to perpetuate — was worth suffering for, are not the scenes through which they passed worthy of commemoration and remembrance in the hearts of their fellow-countrymen? Justice to the living who suffered, impartial history, and the martyred dead, demand a full, unexaggerated record by a survivor of these horrors. For this purpose this book, through agonizing memories, at last has been finished. With the author it has been rather a work of solemn duty than of pleasure. He simply states facts, and depicts those scenes of prison life best fitted to convey to the minds of general readers some of its characteristic phases, just as prisoners saw it,—giving to history material for its verdict, and the reader a full understanding of the subject.

In almost every household throughout the land there are saddened memories of these dreadful prisons; but as terrible as has been the past, thousands of the same patriotic men are ready to spring to arms again for the preservation of national life and honor. On his crutch, the author makes his bow to the public, hoping that in THE SOLDIER'S STORY they may find instruction and profit.

CONTENTS.

———◦◦;◦;◦◦———

CHAPTER I.

CHAPTER II.

CHAPTER III.

CHAPTER IV.

CHAPTER V.

CHAPTER VI.

CHAPTER VII.

CHAPTER VIII.

CHAPTER IX.

CHAPTER X.

CHAPTER XI.

CHAPTER XII.

CHAPTER XIII.

CHAPTER XIV.

INTRODUCTION.

THE world's ear is full of cries from the land of rebel barbarism, where starvation walked at the side of every captive, and suffering, despair, and death sat at every prison door. In these prisons thousands of patriotic hearts ceased to beat during the war that has recently closed. Torn with hunger and hapless despair, they sadly and mournfully died during the long and bitter imprisonments to which rebel cruelty subjected them. Thousands of hearts have bled at the mere recital of the horrors of Libby, Andersonville, Florence, Danville, and Salisbury. And far lands, looking across the ocean, have shuddered at the spectacle of rebel barbarity, developed before their eyes, wondering how in a Christian country such things could be. It is, perhaps, an old story now; but, as no detailed account of any one of great experience has ever been presented to the public by the sufferer himself, the writer of this narrative proposes to tell what he has seen, and felt, and known, of the slaveholders' mercy while yet the touch of their fierce cruelty is upon him.

During the progress of the war, it has been my misfortune to have been twice a prisoner, once in 1862, and again in 1864, — the first period of captivity four months, the second nine months, — making in all over year of the most unparalleled misery which man ever survived. My experience in these prisons was of a kind which few endure and live. Mr. Richardson, the correspondent, who has done so much to enlighten the public mind on this subject, by his own acknowledgment, a great part of his time enjoyed the comparative luxury of a hospital. Sergeant Kellogg, who has written a very true account of his imprisonment at Andersonville, was a sergeant of a hundred men, and drew extra rations; and a good portion of his time was also spent in hospitals of the prisons. Very hard fare was his, it is true, but a luxury to what the great mass of prisoners enjoyed. My imprisonment was without mitigation of this kind, except the last three weeks of my last confinement.

I propose to relate the tale of horrors experienced in these prisons without exaggeration. All language which my poor pen can command is powerless to convey even a faint impression of what men suffered there. Very few went through those imprisonments without becoming idiotic — mere wrecks of humanity, unfit to convey their impressions by reason of weakness of mind, and unwilling, even if they had the power, because of the soul-harrowing, frightful memories which were thus recalled. Therefore it is that the most terrible sufferings have never been delineated, or even attempted. Though it may be presumption in me to attempt it, yet I will try to make the world acquainted with some of the details of prison life and experience. I know how hard it is to realize that men can live through some of the cruelties which I shall relate ; but "truth is stranger than fiction," and no truth is stranger than " man's inhumanity to man," as developed in rebel prisons.

THE SOLDIER'S STORY.

CHAPTER I.

Enlistment in the Engineer Corps. — A Prophecy of Dining in Richmond fulfilled different from Expectations. — Battle at Savage's Station. — Terrible Conflict. — The Army of the Potomac saved. — An Incident. — Heroism in a Wounded Soldier. — A Retreat. — Wounded taken Prisoners. — First Treatment as a Prisoner. — Rebel Prediction of the Capture of Washington. — Confidence in McClellan. — Stonewall Jackson. — False Promises. — Taken to Richmond. — A Sad Scene. — A Rebel Officer's Wit. — A Retort. — Search and Confiscation of Personal Effects. — Description of Prison. — Life in Libby Prison. — Horrors of such Life. — Various Incidents. — Change of Quarters. — Hope for the Better disappointed.

AT an early date in the war, I was a member of the United States engineer corps of the regular army, at that time consisting of one company, and two others partially formed, all under Captain Duane, for some time chief engineer of the army of the Potomac. I performed the usual duties of an engineer at Yorktown, at Williamsburg, and on the Chickahominy, until, being in the first stages of a fever, I was sent to Savage's Station, where I was taken prisoner. About two weeks previous to my being captured,

2

I had written to my friends, that, in course of a week or more, I expected to dine in Richmond. Though it proved to be a *prophecy*, circumstances, in interpreting the language, seemed to have taken me more at my word than at my wish; for it would have been more congenial with the wishes of the prophet to have entered the "city of his hopes" in a very different style than that which fate ordained.

On the 27th of June I arrived at Savage's Station, the sound of battle on every side telling how desperate was the nature of the contest. On the 28th and 29th, the Williamsburg road, which passed the camp near Savage's Station, was crowded with baggage wagons, ammunition, pontoon trains, and all the indescribable material of a vast army. The hospital camp at Savage's Station consisted of three hundred hospital tents and several negro shanties full of sick and wounded soldiers from the battle-fields.

"There is an open plain of several hundred acres opposite Savage's Station. It was along this plain the Williamsburg road passes, by which our troops were mainly to effect their retreat," or change of base. "Beyond the level plain was a dense pine forest." It was here, on the edge of the road, that, on the afternoon of the 29th, General Sumner was stationed with twenty thousand men, who were to hold in check the enemy until our troops had escaped beyond the White Oak Swamp. "Here these men awaited, in one dark mass, for hours, the approach of the trebly outnumbering foe, while regiments, divisions, and trains filed by them. The fate of the army was in their hands, and they proved worthy of the trust."

About five o'clock in the afternoon, dense clouds of dust rising in the wood beyond heralded the approach of the enemy. "As they drew near, from their whole mass of artillery in front they opened a terrific fire, to which our guns responded," until through the dense smoke was seen only the flash of artillery, like lightning from the tempest cloud. Sometimes the roar of the conflict would almost cease, but only to be renewed with more terrible vigor. "For an hour not a musket was discharged, but the reverberating thunder of the cannon shook the hills; then the whole majestic mass of rebels," with their peculiar yell, in marked contrast with the three distinct cheers of our men, "sprang forward upon the plain, presenting a crested billow of glittering bayonets, which, it would seem, no mortal power could withstand. Every musket in the Union lines was brought into deliberate aim. For a moment, there was a pause, until it was certain that every bullet would fulfil its mission, and then a flash, followed by a storm of lead, which covered the ground with dead and dying." The three distinct cheers of our men responded to the hyena-like yell of the rebels. Beaten back by this storm of lead, the rebel host wavered, broke, and retreated to the railroad. Troops coming up behind pressed them forward again to our lines. "Again there leaped from ten thousand guns the fiery blast, and yell

answered yell; for a moment a pause, to be succeeded by the instantaneous discharge of ten thousand
guns." And then, as if stung to frenzy, the rage of
the conflict was redoubled — the clash of arms interrupted by the occasional arrival of reënforcements in
the field on the rebel side, who, as they came up,
cheered their companions with loud shouts.

The battle raged incessantly until half past eight or
nine o'clock, when cheer after cheer went up from our
men, to which was heard no answering rebel yell, telling
that the army of the Potomac was saved. The rebels
brought into the field fifty thousand men, and were
beaten back by the gallant, devoted men under Sumner.

During the action, and afterwards, I was rendering
to the wounded such assistance as it was in my power
to contribute. At one time, while aiding a young surgeon (whose name I did not learn) who was ampu-
tating a limb, as I turned aside to obtain water for
his use, the surgeon and patient were both killed and
terribly mutilated by the explosion of a shell.

On the battle-field one sometimes hears sentiments
from the rough soldier which would do credit to the
most refined and chivalrous. At Savage's Station a
young soldier belonging, I think, to the fifteenth
Massachusetts regiment, was brought in wounded, had
his wound dressed, and lay with closed eyes, apparently
thinking. Presently he began to talk with me and
others. "I have been thinking," said he, "how proud
I shall be some day of these scars" (placing his hand

upon the dressing of the terrible sabre wound he had received across the face). "How proud my mother will be of them!" Suddenly the terrible discharge of artillery brought him to his feet. "Where is my rifle?" inquired he. "Surely," said one, "you will not go into the fight wounded as you are!" He turned his large, intelligent eye upon the speaker, and, with an expression on his face I never can forget, in those low, suppressed tones which men sometimes use when keeping down or repressing excitement, said, while he buckled on his war harness, "Look yonder! On the hill-side is the flag of my brigade, and I never could forgive myself if I neglected this chance to render service to my country." He went, and my heart went with him. I saw him reach and mingle with his comrades in time to take part in the conflict.

It was no wonder we were victorious, no wonder that the rebel hosts were driven back, and that there came no answering yell to the cheers of victory from the Union army; for our army was made up of patriotic material — men who perilled life for their good government — the material to wring victory from defeat! Hence, too, it was, that our army, though retreating and outnumbered, whipped the enemy in almost every battle during the seven days' fighting which terminated at Malvern Hill. After the battle of Savage's Station, says the Rev. Mr. Marks, "General Sumner called for reënforcements to drive the enemy into the Chickahominy, thus showing how complete was our victory."

When this conflict was over, worn and exhausted with sickness and my exertions, yet content in the conviction that the victory was ours, I wrapped myself in my blanket and slept soundly, but awoke in the morning to find myself a prisoner. Our force had retreated during the night, leaving the whole hospital camp at Savage's Station prisoners in the hands of the enemy. The first intimation was on finding a rebel guard around the camp. During the three or four days we remained here, the treatment experienced in the main was good, although no attention was given us, such as providing rations and medicines. Even our ice, of which there was a meagre quantity for the wounded, was taken by the rebel authorities, and sent to Richmond for the use of the Confederate sick and wounded. The enemy whom we came in contact with from the battle-fields, as a general thing, treated us kindly, or rather let us alone.

As an instance of coolness manifested by our wounded at this time, I recollect one soldier desperately wounded in the leg, who had taken up his abode under a large tree near the station. He was as merry as a cricket, cracked jokes, whistled, and sang, and whittled like a veritable Yankee, as he doubtless was. A Union surgeon gave him some ice one day to put on his wound to prevent mortification, for the heat was intense. The poor fellow eyed the ice, and commenced eating it, and at last had eaten all except a small piece, when he began to look first at his leg and then at the ice, as if doubtful whether to finish eating the ice or to use it to cool his leg. He hesitated but a moment, and then said to himself, "G—d, I guess I'll eat it all and let it 'strike out.'"

Several correspondents of the Richmond press visited us at Savage's Station. "Our army," said one of them to me, casually, while taking notes, "will be in Washington in a few days." I could not refrain from answering the boast, by saying, "Undoubtedly, but they will go there as I shall go to Richmond soon." And such was my confidence in McClellan at that time, that I fully believed him to be manœuvring to bag the whole rebel army. The correspondent, after recommending me to keep a civil tongue in my head, turned sneeringly away.

About the same time, a seedy-looking officer rode up, whom I accosted with the question of how we were to be sent into Richmond. "In ambulances," said he. "That," said a rebel guard, as the officer rode away, "is Jackson, our general." True enough, as I ascertained afterwards, it was Stonewall Jackson, who proved himself, in the few words of conversation I held with him, to be as big a liar as the rest of the rebels I had met; for he must have known that the rebel army were greatly deficient in the article for the use of their wounded.

On the 5th July, we were packed into filthy cattle cars, the sick and wounded crowded together, and sent into Richmond. About twenty of our wounded are said to have died during the passage of little over one hour. Arriving at the depot in Richmond, we were formed in order around the canal, preparatory to marching to prison. We were a hard-looking crowd, made greatly so through suffering. The heat of the day was such as to make the thinnest garment intolerable. Many cast away their shirts and coats, and others their pantaloons and shoes. "So many wounded and sick men in the streets of the rebel capital, pale, bleeding, and in some cases nearly naked, starting on their march for the prison"—an imprisonment which, with the great majority, ended only with death—was calculated to excite pity in the hardest heart.

Many were hopping on rude crutches; others, with amputated arms and shattered shoulders, moved as far as possible from their staggering companions, and were constantly pressed back into the surging mass by the bayonets of the brutal guard. Several blind men were guided by the arms of the wounded, who leaned upon them for support. Others, confused and uncertain, groped and staggered every step like the palsied. "Here," says Rev. Mr. Marks, who was a witness of the scene, "one, wounded in the leg, had thrown away his torn and bloody pants, and was limping along with nothing but his crimson bandages; another, wounded in the chest and arm, had thrown off his blood-stiffened shirt, and, with the upper portion of the body bare, moved along in the crowd, leaning upon a less injured companion."

Such was the crowd that left the depot and slowly moved around the canal. One would think such a

" Many were hopping on rude crutches; others, with amputated arms and shattered shoulders, moved as far as possible from their staggering companions, and were constantly pressed back into the surging mass by the bayonets of the brutal guard." — Page 24.

spectacle was calculated to excite pity, but in this case it excited scoffs and derision. Even the children took the tone of their elders, and one little fellow, about six years of age, perched exultantly upon a gate, condensed in the single sentence of, "We've got you, you d—d Yankees you!" a whole volume of rebel hate and triumph. If we did not then believe ourselves to be that description of a Yankee, we had occasion to change our opinion when we arrived at our destination. On our way an officer rode up to us, tinselled with gold lace in a most extraordinary manner, — doubtless some officer of the home guard, — and sneering, asked if that was "Falstaff's army of recruits!" "No," replied one of the boys at my side, who understood the insult, "we are not; but here they come;" pointing to a detachment of dilapidated rebels coming around a corner with the shuffling, unmilitary gait which is peculiar to the Johnnies. The officer rode away without any more attempts at wit.

In the mean time, the sidewalks were lined with citizens who came to see the "Yanks," as they would to the exhibition of some strange animal. A very few exhibited any pity. A few women — mostly Irish or German — gave us food at the risk of their lives. While we halted before the prison, on Cary Street, the shades of night had come over the city. Many of the sick and wounded had fallen upon the pavements and sidewalks from sheer exhaustion. After remaining two hours before prison No. 2, on Cary Street, we were ordered in, and there went through with the ceremony of being searched. Everything the chivalry took a fancy to was confiscated as contraband. Not even my jackknife and comb escaped, and I found myself, after the search, destitute of every thing but my blanket and the clothes on my back.

The prison was one of the large tobacco warehouses, three stories high; the rooms were large, poorly ventilated, and disgustingly filthy. The dust and tobacco juice of years had gathered in hillocks and ridges over the floor. These apartments were indescribably foul. They had been filled with prisoners who had but just been removed to make room for us, and had left behind them all the offal of mortal maladies, weakness, and wounds. There had been no sweeping or cleaning, but into these rooms we were forced, compelled to drink in the suffocating air, the first breath of which caused one to shudder.

The room in which I, with about two hundred of my companions, was placed, was too filthy for description. Here, for five days, almost suffocating from want of air, and crowded for room, I remained, having rations issued to me only twice during the five days, and those poor in quality, and insufficient in quantity for a sick man. So with all the sick and wounded. No medical attention was given, and the horror of our situation seemed more than could be borne. To such a degree were we crowded, that we were obliged to arrange ourselves in tiers, like pins on paper, when we slept at night. And even with this precaution we were crowded for sleeping-room. Constant interference of some one's feet with another's head or shins caused such continued wrangling as to make night and day more like an abode of fiends than one of human beings.

At last I was taken from this place, and sent to Libby Prison, which has often been described; and yet from the description given, no adequate idea of the sufferings endured can be formed. The filth and heat were greater than even the place I had left. With some five hundred others I was crowded into the garret, next the roof, of the prison. The hot sun, beating down upon the roof, made the filthy garret, crowded with men clamoring for standing-room, suffocating in a degree which one cannot well understand who never experienced it. During the day, in the corners of our garret the dead remained among the living, and from these through all the rooms came the pestilent breath of a charnel-house. The vermin swarmed in every crack and crevice; the floors had not been cleaned for years. To consign men to such quarters was like signing their death warrant. Two men were shot by the rebel guard while trying to get breath at the windows.

The third day of my confinement in this abode of torture, I noticed a young soldier dying: his long, fair hair was matted in the indescribable liquid filth and dirt which clotted and ran over the floor of the prison. He was covered with vermin; the flies had gathered on his wasted hands, on his face, and in the sunken sockets of his eyes. But even in this condition hunger had not left him. The scene seemed to fascinate me, and in spite of the repulsiveness of the picture, I continued to look upon it, though it was much against my will. I saw him try to get to his mouth a dirty piece of bread, which he held in his hand : the effort was in vain ; the hand fell nerveless by his side ; a convulsive shudder, and he was dead. After he had been dead half an hour, his hand still clasped over the poor dirty piece of bread, a Zouave who had one leg amputated, observing the bread, dragged himself through the filth and dirt, and unclasping the dead man's fingers, took the bread from the rigid hand, and ate it like a famished wolf.

Men lay on the filthy floor unable to help themselves, gasping for breath, while their more healthy companions trod upon and stumbled over them. The common expression used was, "I shall die unless I get fresh air." Every breath they breathed was loaded with the poison of fever and the effluvia of the dead. When rations were issued, two thirds of the very sick got nothing, for the manner of issuing was without order, and the distribution was by a general scramble among those who were the best able to wrangle for it. I was fortunate in getting rations the first day in Libby, but the second and third I got none. Meanwhile, my fever grew worse and worse ; oppressed for breath, crowded for room, unable to get into the prison yard to perform the common functions of nature, to which was added the want of medicines and even common food, made my situation so horribly intolerable that I could only hope for relief in death. All this was made worse by the constant wrangling for room, for air, and food. I succeeded in obtaining some pieces of board, by which means I raised myself from the dirty floor and the liquid filth around me.

I had been in Libby about a week, when an officer passed through the rooms, announcing that those who were able to walk could be accommodated with quarters in a healthy location on Belle Island. None of us had heard of Belle Island as a prison at that time, and we were eager to better our condition. Worse it did not seem possible it could be, and we believed there would be some truth even with rebels in dealing with men in our situation. The chance of benefiting myself was irresistible, and so I managed to crawl and stumble down stairs into the streets. The breathing of fresh air once more was refreshing; but, trying to get into line, I stumbled, and fell fainting to the ground. I was carried by some kind people into an Irishwoman's shop, where I was treated to raspberry wine and baker's bread. She asked me if I thought our army would come into Richmond. I answered her (believing it true), that I thought our army would have Richmond in a week or two. "I hope they will," said she; "for this is a devilish place, and I wish I was in New York." I got into line after being persuaded by the bayonet of the guard, and, being too weak to stand, fell down on the pavement. A rebel guard, addressing me, said, "I guess you'd better not go down there, old hoss; Belle Isle's a right smart hard place, and I *reckon* you won't any more'n live to get down thar any way." About the time we commenced our line of march for Belle Isle, it began to rain in torrents, drenching me through. I should never have reached the prison camp alive, had it not been for the kind assistance tendered me by the rebel soldier who had previously addressed me as "old hoss."

We arrived at one of the long bridges which cross the James River between Belle Isle and Richmond; after which I have a confused recollection of falling, succeeded by a blank. I knew no more, until I found myself lying on the damp ground, with no shelter from the driving rain, and hundreds of others around me in the same situation. I have only a confused recollection of what occurred for four or five days after my arrival, when I inquired where I was. I was addressed as "old crazy" by my companions, and told to keep still. I afterwards learned that I had been delirious most of the time for four or five days, during which I had received no medical attention or care except the cold-water cure of nature. This came in such copious quantities as to remind one of what is related of Charles Lamb, who, on being questioned concerning the cold-water cure, replied that he never knew where it had been tried on an extensive principle since the deluge, when he believed it killed more than it cured.

It was three weeks before I got a shelter, though there were quite a number of tents on the Island; and the shelter which I became possessed of consisted of an old striped bedtick ripped open, and set upon sticks, in poor imitation of an A tent.

CHAPTER II.

Belle Island. — Sickness and Insensibility. — Want of Medical
Treatment. — Description of Belle Isle Prison. — Strict Regulations evaded. — Trading with the Rebels. — Insufficiency of Food.
— High Prices of Commissary Stores. — Depreciated and Coun-
terfeit Currency. — Comparative Virtue and Intelligence of Rebels
of different States. — Extreme Suffering from Hunger. — Effects
on the Character. — Philosophy on the Subject. — A Goose Question. — Exchange on the Brain. — Increased Mortality. — A Gleam
of Hope. — Exchange and Disappointment. — Escape and its Punishment. — A Rebel Admission that Richmond might have been
captured by McClellan. — More Prisoners and Suffering. — Exchange. — Sight of the Old Flag.

BELLE ISLAND is situated on a bend of the James
River, about half a mile west of Richmond. The
river at this point is very swift of current, and full of
fantastic groups of rocks and little islands, covered with
luxuriant foliage, among which the water dashes in
sparkling foam. Three bridges span the river between
the island and the city. The island contains some
forty or fifty superficial acres, rises at the lower extremity, towards Richmond, in a gentle, sandy plain,
and upon this was situated the prison camp, consisting
of about four acres of the lowest land on the James
River — almost on a level with the river, and conse-

quently unhealthy.   Beyond the prison grounds to the
westward the island rises into a precipitous bluff, there
crowned by strong earthworks, which commanded the
river above.   The prison grounds were surrounded by
a low board railing, around which guards were stationed at intervals of fifteen paces.

The guard regulations on the island were very strict.
The rules established were, that there should be no conversation between the prisoners and the guard, and that
no prisoner was to come within three feet of the railing
or fence which enclosed the prison.   But, in spite of
rules and regulations, the irresistible Yankee spirit of
trade and dicker perverted even the virtuous grayback
guardians of the prison.   Trading over the line on the
sly was one of the professions, and all became more or
less expert at the business.   As the guard had orders
to shoot or bayonet any one infringing these rules, the
business was sometimes risky, especially when a new
guard was put on who knew not the ways of those who
were before them, when some contrary Secesh was on
duty who did not care to learn, or some confiding individual of the grayback species who had been cheated in
a sharp trading speculation.

The common way in opening negotiations for trade
with a new or ugly guard was to hold up, at a safe distance, some article of a tempting nature, — a jackknife,
watch, or a pair of boots, — making signs that they
were to be purchased cheap, until the virtuous Secesh
broke the ice by inquiring the price.   A lookout being

3

established to give warning of the approach of the officers of the guard, trade would commence, and spread from guard to guard, and sometimes beyond the guard all along the line. In this manner a whole guard would be seduced from virtue, and put to silence by the fascination of high-top Yankee boots and pinchbeck watches. The commodities of trade on the Yankee side were articles of clothing which could ill be afforded, bone rings of prison manufacture, watches, chains, and jackknives; the last-named being temptations against which the most obdurate of Johnnies was not proof. Even a commissioned officer would condescend to chaffer and trade for a pair of boots or a jackknife. In return, we were the recipients of hoe-cake, wood to cook with, apples, and sometimes potatoes and tobacco. Occasionally officers from Richmond came into the prison, and traded for clothing, and were not too honest sometimes to walk off without paying for their purchases.

I had been steadily getting up from the fever which had prostrated me, the turning-point of which occurred during my first week's experience at "Belle Isle," when I gradually regained strength, though the food was so insufficient and poor as to reduce the inmates of the prison to an almost starving condition. I found by personal experience and observation that, when hungry, men will adopt very ungenteel habits to satisfy their cravings, such as picking up bones rejected by others, and gnawing them like dogs, struggling for stray potato peelings, in fact, anything of an eatable nature.

I saw one day an Irish acquaintance who had possessed himself of a bacon bone with some meat on it, but more maggots than meat. "What are you doing, Jim?" I interrogated. "Quarrelling with the maggots," said Pat, with a comic leer, "to see who will have the bone." Whereupon he brushed the maggots off, contemptuously, and went in for a meal.

Our rations at this time consisted of one half loaf to each man per day, and beans, cooked in water in which bacon had been boiled for the guard, — usually containing about twenty per cent. of maggots, — owing to scarcity of salt; thirty per cent. of beans, and the remainder in water. There may have been a very small percentage of salt, but the fact was not ascertainable by the sense of taste. Only through faith — which could give no great flavor to the palate — could one see its existence in the soup — for such was the name with which this compound was dignified. It was issued sometimes twice a week, and sometimes not at all. The bread was of a very good quality, but so spongy that our poor daily half loaf could be enclosed in the half shut hand. The insufficiency of food was aggravated by neglect of the prison authorities to issue regularly; sometimes we got no rations from Saturday morning until Monday night. The excuse usually given was, that the bakers in the city were on a drunk, or that there were no blank requisitions, which excuses

didn't seem to fill our stomachs, and though they had
to be taken in place of rations, we found them a poor
substitute.   No "back rations" were ever issued.

The buildings of the commissary department were
just outside the prison limits, near the water's edge, on
the south side.   Here non-commissioned officers of the
prison, having charge of the issue of rations, were called
out, when the bread was counted out to them and
brought in in blankets.   The fact that these blankets
were infested with vermin did not detract from the
tremendous cravings of appetite.   At the commissary's, molasses, pies, and sugar were kept for sale
at exorbitant rates — molasses, one dollar per pint,
sugar, one dollar and fifty cents per pound, onions,
twenty-five cents apiece, and every thing else pro-
portionally high.   Butter and milk could rarely be
had at any price.   Though not acknowledging any
superiority, at that time, of the value of greenbacks
over their shinplaster currency, they much preferred
the former, in payment, to their own.   It was quite
noticeable that they showed a good deal of hesita-
tion in taking their own scrip.   Their fractional currency consisted of bills issued by cities, towns, and
private individuals.   Petersburg money, or the fractional currency of any other town, would not pass current.   On the sly, even at that date, rebel officers would
buy up greenbacks at the rate of three dollars for one.
Fellows in our condition developed some talents, which
under other circumstances, and among decent people,

would have been considered dangerous. Two dollar
greenbacks were altered into twenties, ones into tens,
&c.   Broken down banks of northern States were
passed by us, and received with grasping eagerness,
and even rebel shinplasters were changed into higher
denominations than they were ever intended to repre-
sent.   Counterfeited brass was also worked up into
heavy gold chains by ingenious Yankees.   In fact,
every means, however desperate, was resorted to, all
for the purpose of obtaining food.   Except in some
very rare cases, we did not swindle the rebel guard,
which would have been for our disadvantage.   But
woe to the unsuspecting citizen, who, in his greed of
gain, seduced the virtuous (?) graybacks to enable him
to trade over their post with the Yanks.

As soon as I obtained sufficient strength to walk
round, I entered into competition with others, and
after trading away my shoes and coat for food, set up
as a kind of commission merchant, for dealing in boots
and any other article of clothing of trading value.   By
this means, with perseverance I managed occasionally
to obtain an extra johnny-cake, a potato, or an onion.
I might have been seen at any time during the day
passing slowly around the guard line, trying to strike
up a trade for something to eat.   In passing thus around
the camp, I had a chance to become acquainted with
the disposition of the guard belonging to different
States.   I found the Alabama and Georgia men to be
the most intelligent, while the rank and file belonging

to Virginia regiments were the most ignorant and vindictive. A common question proposed to me was, " What do you'uns come down to fight we'uns for?" It was of no use to state facts, however impartial, or to argue, for it would only bring a repetition of the same question. They seemed to be oblivious of the fact that the quarrel was commenced by themselves, and any instructions volunteered by a Yank would be argued by the angry thrust of the bayonet, which was too powerful an argument to be met; consequently the Johnny considered himself a victor in all argument, since where he failed in reason, he parried with the less sentimental but more powerful argument of force, which has always seemed to me to be the distinctive method adopted by the two sections. It makes, in the end, however, but little difference, as they have been soundly beaten with their own favorite arguments of force, which they applied indiscriminately to the heads of our legislators before the war, and during its progress to prisoners of war and non-combatants.

During the last of July our sufferings were intense. All other thoughts and feelings had become concentrated in that of hunger. Even home was associated only with the various descriptions of good food. John H——, a sergeant of the eighteenth Massachusetts, used to answer my questions of how he was, with the invariable expression, "Hungry as h—ll," which may have been correct, as far as torment of that description exists in the place mentioned. There were three stages of hunger in my experience; first, the common hungry craving one experiences after missing his dinner and supper; second, this passed away, and was succeeded by headache and a gnawing at the stomach; then came weakness, trembling of the limbs, which, if not relieved by food, was followed by death. Ordinarily we received just enough food to keep us hungry, which may seem a doubtful expression to the general reader; but those who have been similarly circumstanced, who read this, will recognize it as a truth. Men became, under such surroundings, indifferent to almost everything, except their own miseries, and found an excuse in their sufferings for any violations of the ordinary usages of humanity. An incident occurred illustrative of this which came to my notice while I was trading around the camp.

Near the dead line, on the west side of the camp, were one or two wild-cherry trees, which formed the only shade in the prison limits, and these not much, as, from time to time, their branches had been cut off for fuel, in spite of the vigilance of the guard, and the necessity of shade for the prisoners. Here, one afternoon, I found a German dying. No one was there to care for him and soothe his dying moments; the parched, filthy ground was his death-bed; over his wasted hands and sunken face the flies were gathering, while the disgusting sores of his flesh swarmed with maggots and other vermin. Moved by such a spectacle, I sat down by his side to brush the flies from his pallid face, and moisten the parched lips with water from my canteen. Quite a number thereupon gathered around. One, professing sympathy with so pitiable an object, suggested that he would feel better to have his boots off, and forthwith pulling them off, coolly walked away with them, and sold them. I afterwards met and recognized him, and expressed very freely my opinion that he had been guilty of a detestable act, unworthy of anything human. He confessed that it was rather rough, but excused himself by saying he was hungry, and thought it not so bad to steal from a dying man as from one likely to live; and he thought the boots would do him more good than a dead man. There was some show of reason in this, and so much effrontery that I made no reply.

Different minds are no doubt affected in a different degree by prison life, which in its best phase is simply inhuman, unnatural. But whatever the mental constitution, it must be influenced to a certain degree by terrible sufferings, and deflected, as it were, from its habitual angle. It is the calm, phlegmatic man of philosophical balance, who is best calculated to endure, to look at the best side of every misfortune, and who brings to his aid the reflection that every moment is complete in itself, and adopts for his motto in all his sufferings "Sufficient unto the moment is the evil thereof." One who is naturally ill-tempered, under the aggravations of imprisonment becomes an insupportable monster. But if bad qualities are so forcibly developed

in some, the good also in others expands in the same
ratio. The generous carry liberality into improvi-
dence, while the charitable become self-sacrificing in
their bounty. Suffering develops real character; dis-
guise throws off its mask under bodily and mental
anguish, unreservedly, and indeed unawares, and shows
the true character. Suffering is the crucible of human
metal, and pure indeed must be the gold which is not
tarnished or turned to dross by the heat of unmitigated
afflictions. Under the tortures of imprisonment, that
goodness must indeed be real which never forgets itself,
but stands firmly upon its pedestal to the last.

I was mixed up in some "right smart tall grass," as
the expression goes among the "rebs," on account of
the stealing of a Secesh goose. As the circumstances
are illustrative of the risks men were willing to run in
order to obtain food, although trivial I will relate them.
A squad of geese belonging to the Secesh officers were
often on parade just outside of prison limits, headed by
a gander who seemed to take some pride in the dis-
cipline and organization of his fellows — their drill and
marching being fully equal, if not superior to that of
their owners — the Secesh. The mouths of the prisoners often watered at the bare thought of a boiled
goose. One evening, about sundown, while the attention of the sentinel was occupied with trade, the unsuspecting geese were enticed under the guard railing with
corn, a dash was made, and a goose and gander were
captured. Their necks were wrung in a hurry. The

cackling was drowned by some unusual noise furnished for the purpose, and although the guard mistrusted "something was up," they did not find out the secret until next morning, when it was ascertained and particularly noticed that "goosy, goosy gander, no more did wander," and was missed from his accustomed haunts. Meanwhile, the goose had been eaten, without salt or sauce, and relished immensely. I was suspected of being concerned; but although many inquiries and threats were made, the inquirers were no wiser nor sounder on the "goose question" than before. Our conscience did not trouble us, for had it not been written, "Rebel property shall be confiscated."

The 1st of August developed a fearful epidemic in prison, known as Exchange on the Brain. The symptoms among those infected were, they were continually rushing around camp, with the very latest news about exchange, to the great neglect of their personal cleanliness, and their skirmishing duties (a term usually applied to the act of hunting for vermin, a partial hunt being termed driving in the pickets). The victims of this epidemic were willing to bet on being exchanged "to-morrow;" their hopes were raised high during the day, followed by a corresponding depression, on the morrow, at being disappointed. With an anxious, haggard look, inquiring of every one who would listen, "What about exchange?" and, thus inquiring, would before noon obtain information (?) which would raise their expectations to a high pitch, to be followed by despondency and discouragement, and sometimes death. The best philosophy was neither to believe nor doubt, but to wait patiently and hope much in a general manner, without setting the heart upon any particular time for its fulfilment.

The contemplation of misery teaches the necessity of hope; cut off from comforts and tender sympathies, from the daily intercourse with friends, from the habitual avocations of life, — shut out from social pleasures, doomed to mental and physical sufferings, to the lethargy of the heart, — he is lost, indeed, who loses hope. But while preserving hope, we should not build expectations on frail foundations and in disappointments lose it. While some of the prisoners endeavored by all sorts of ingenious stratagems to divert their minds from ennui and the monotony and misery of captivity, others gave up to sorrow, and pined away in the midst of morbid reflections and dismal forebodings. Some would lie for hours reading and re-reading old letters, which had perhaps been their companions in peril; and now, as they re-peruse them, were brought back slumbering recollections of home. In the species of existence which the prisoner leads, the memories of the past, the kindly sympathies expressed in tender messages of the dear ones far away in the sphere of real life, the affectionate tokens which he carries with him warm from the heart of unforgotten friends, — all these seem but the echoes of familiar voices borne from another world. They discourse to him pleasantly of departed joys, and past happy hours. There is a piteous consolation in it, like the mournful solace of the remembrance of friends who plant a dear grave with flowers.

Prisoners gather together in groups, as evening comes on, to talk of home, and while away the tedium of the hour by recalling the pleasure which once was theirs; the pleasures of the table were uppermost in their thoughts; the eager attention given when some favorite dish was described in its minutest details, attested the interest taken in everything eatable. Upon lying down at night, the talk was of what we had eaten in times past, and what we would have when we could get it. Suffering as we were from hunger, the sum total of all joy seemed to be condensed in the one act of eating. Some of the prisoners employed their moments in making finger rings of bone, handkerchief slides, napkin rings, watch seals, &c., many of which were very fine, and were bought up by the ' Sesesh ' guard to be sent home as specimens of " Yankee fixings,"as they termed them.

Our fare daily grew worse, and new prisoners coming in, the prison was crowded in such a manner that it seemed impossible to get around. Deaths increased in prison to such a degree that a load of bread for the living was usually accompanied by a load of coffins for the dead. The coffins were of rough pine boards, the only decent thing provided for the prisoners. Rumors of exchange, which flooded the camp, were listened to only by a credulous few, the

thoughts of the majority being cast in that rigid mould
of philosophy which teaches us not so much to fly
from the evils that beset us, as to grapple with them
and trample them under foot — a system of ethics
which, however admirable, it is not easy to follow.

Suddenly a gleam of hope burst upon the wretched
camp of prisoners, and the horizon of prison life is
made bright by the certainty of exchange. Officers
came into the prison and made the announcement, and
we all were excited with the joyful prospect of exchange. On this occasion of exchange, the rebels
prided themselves on the performance of what they
termed a "Yankee trick," in order to get all the men who
were not sick separated from those who were not able
to travel, and by this means they saved themselves much
trouble. All the men who could not march seven miles
were ordered to pass outside of prison bounds with their
blankets and canteens, haversacks, and such rations as
they might have on hand, intimating that such were to
be sent by some mode of conveyance to City Point to
be exchanged. There was a general rush to go out
with those who were thus designated. Many good stout
men, who might easily have marched twice the distance
required, desirous of getting home, scrambled for a
place among cripples and invalids. After lying all
night, waiting with the highest expectations, we awoke
in the morning to find that those who remained in camp
had been marched out for exchange; and we were sent
back, after being kept in a broiling sun a large portion

of the day. In common with the rest, I was disheartened, and men wept like children at this bitter disappointment. I had not, however, the reflection of regret, which many had, who could have marched the required distance.

About half the camp had been exchanged, which in one respect was beneficial to those remaining. We had more room and better quarters. Though our accommodations were better, and for the first time during my imprisonment I had the pleasure of living under a tent, the food became daily worse, less in quantity, and poorer in quality. To make our wretchedness greater, the rations intended for us were sold at the commissary's; and in this manner, for a time, about a third of the men each day were cheated out of their food. The law would not allow the Confederate commissary to take greenbacks; so he employed Yankee prisoners to sell for him, and they became engaged in the transactions of cheating and stealing from their more miserable companions. Such men were generally despised by their comrades for the crouching, cringing subserviency with which they identified themselves with the rebels, upholding and subscribing to their sentiments.

The nights and mornings now became cold, and men who had disposed of their clothes during the warmest weather, sadly felt the need of them. Suffering from cold nights and during rainy weather, was severe, and told terribly on the health of those who, unfortunately, had given way to hunger, and sold their clothing for food. It is hard, however, to determine whether they would have suffered more to have been deprived of the food thus obtained or from the deprivation of garments. Death was almost certain to him who got no food except that furnished by the prison authorities.

Thus affairs became so desperate that, though surrounded by a vigilant guard, and on three sides with water, men were continually trying to make their escape. An Irishman, trying to escape, swam the river, evaded the bullets by diving and good fortune, and reached unhurt the opposite shore. There he was caught and brought into the guard quarters near the prison, and a double guard was established for his safe keeping. To punish him for his attempt at escape, he was "bucked," when he let loose such a piece of his mind, and such a rating with the unruly member, telling his tormentors more truth than they cared to hear, that they gagged him to keep him still. Thus they kept him in a burning sun, until he bled at the mouth and fainted. As soon as he recovered, the gag being removed, nothing daunted, he again gave them a "bit of his mind." They tried to make him clean their rusty guns, but he would not; and they resorted again to the torture. What finally became of him I do not know; but I heard the rumor, of which I have but a little doubt, that he died during the night from cruelty experienced at the hands of his relentless enemies.

On the 1st of September, the guard, which had consisted chiefly of Alabama and Georgia regiments, were sent away, and were relieved by citizens from Richmond, many of them boys not over thirteen years of age, who could hardly carry a musket. One of these citizen soldiers one day ran a bayonet through a New York boy, from the effects of which he died in a few hours. A soldier of the Hawkins Zouaves sprang at the guard, and, reaching over the railing, seized him by the throat, lifted him from the ground, shook him until the "rebel brave" was black in the face, then hurled him from him like a dog. The officer of the guard, coming up at the time, was saluted with a brick, which knocked him down. When inquiries were instituted, no information was to be got inside the prison. No one knew who threw the brick, or choked the guard! I ever found our foreign soldiers in prison among the most inveterate haters of rebels, and unyielding as iron. During the last of August and first of September, no less than eight men were killed by the rebel guard.

Captain Montgomery at that time was in command of the rebel post at Belle Island. In conversation with him one day, he remarked that, after the battle of Fair Oaks, our forces might have taken Richmond; that there was a panic among their troops, through apprehension of our following up the advantage gained during the last day's fight; and that the James River bridges had been got ready to be destroyed by fire. He seemed very inquisitive about public sentiment at the North, and as to how long the North would fight.

Some two thousand prisoners were added to our

number from Salisbury during September. They had been much better fed than ourselves, and were much dirtier, having been deprived of the advantages of water, which we had from the river, and from little shallow wells from five to eight feet deep, which we dug all over the prison grounds. Several officers accompanied them, among whom was Colonel Corcoran, who, with other commissioned officers, was sent over to Richmond. After this arrival of prisoners, we were again crowded for room; and the hopes of another exchange had almost died out, when our camp was flooded with rumors of release by parole. Day after day passed. Hunger-stricken and pinched with cold, these walking spectres wandered around camp, gathering in groups to talk of home and exchange.

About this time I got a Richmond paper, which argued that dirty people required less food than people who were clean, instancing the Yankee prisoners of Belle Isle as an illustration of the truth of the assumption. Another paragraph announced that prisoners at Belle Isle would be exchanged on the coming Tuesday. Tuesday came, but no parole or exchange! We waited patiently, in hopes that something might turn up to relieve us; but no relief came. It was so hard to wait, even a few days, for relief from our condition, that the uncertainty to which everything in rebeldom seemed condemned was excruciating mental torment, added to the physical misery endured. This jumbling together of so much of hopeless mortality, this endless crash of

4

matter and ceaseless shock of tortured humanity, is a curse to the mind. Some were on the "tip-toe" of expectation; others, in their gloomy despondency, were resigned to the desperate idea of making a winter of it in this dreadful place, when a bow of promise appeared upon the dark background of adversity that overshadowed the prison, and a bright day of deliverance dawned upon us.

The dark night of misery passed away, and I was called out to write in paroling the prisoners. With eager, trembling hand, I wrote first my own parole, and then worked all night. There were some funny descriptions accompanying the paroles — for instance, red hair, blue eyes, and dark complexion. Before morning the blanks of liberty were made out, and as morning dawned, we all hurried out of prison, — a motley crowd, ragged, dirty, and famine-stricken.

The sick took fresh courage, and under Freedom's inspiration the lame walked, and rejoiced that their term of captivity was ended; that once again they were to be under the protecting folds of Liberty's starry banner. Again we entered Richmond; and, as we passed through its streets, skeletons in form, from which almost all semblance of humanity had fled under the torture of imprisonment, we excited pity among even the virulent women of the capital. They filled our canteens with water, and their kind faces showed that they were not dead to all pity. This revulsion of feeling in our favor since first passing through the rebel capital, was caused, perhaps, by their own sufferings — the loss of some father or brother. Be it as it may, I know that while the expressions of hate were few, the kindly expressions were many in our behalf. Perhaps·military restrictions were removed, which before had checked expression, and the rebel authorities were willing we should have some kindly remembrances upon our departure from such scenes. The shops of the city had mostly been closed, and one of the guard told me that every house in Richmond was either a prison or a hospital. Though this may have been exaggeration, it was no doubt a fact that all the dwellings of Richmond had their spare rooms occupied by Confederate sick and wounded. In this city the infantry guards were relieved, and a cavalry escort furnished, who showed their confidence in our desire to reach our lines by letting us straggle as we had a mind to.

During the day we marched without food, and finally, late in the afternoon, a feeble cheer went up from the advance, which told that the old flag on our transports was in sight. Need I say how wildly our hearts beat at sight of that dear old flag which we had followed in battle, and which had floated among the peaceful scenes of home! The feeling was too deep to be expressed in words or cheers. Tears of joy started to eyes unused to weep at misery; the voice that attempted expression was lost in choking sobs. Men sat quietly down, tears coursing their dirt-furrowed cheeks, contented to look up and see the "old flag" floating over them.   I sat in this manner, having, without knowing it, a quiet, joyful cry, when a comrade came along, inquiring, " What are you blubbering about, old fellow ? "   I looked up, and saw he hadn't much to brag about, and replied, that I was crying because folks were such fools as to live under a flag · with three stripes, when they might have one with thirteen over them.

We hoisted anchor, left those scenes, and came, at last, a sick, maimed, emaciated company, to Annapolis. There kind hands cared for us, kind welcomes cheered us, and we knew we were at home at last—at home with the arms of a great nation around us, with the great love of noble loyal hearts.   When I left Belle Island I had no hair or hat on my head, and my clothing consisted only of a pair of pantaloons and a shirt.   Neither hat, shoes, or jacket had I.

CHAPTER III.

THREE months followed in the parole camp, where
I regained strength; and the hardships through
which I had passed seemed rather a distorted dream
than a dreadful reality. Does the mind lose the sharp
impressions of hardships, that it is inclined to look
upon the pleasures rather than upon the dangers and
disagreeable incidents of the past? I will not tire the
reader with details of incidents which in a few months
ended in my discharge for disability, resulting from
injuries received in the line of duty.

Once more I returned to my home, where its comforts and kind friends contributed to my restoration to health. Possessed naturally of a strong constitution, I recovered with almost marvellous quickness from disabilities which an able board of medical men had pronounced incurable. With returning health came the desire to be again with my companions in the field. The clash of arms, the excitement of battle, the hurried military parades and displays, awoke all the pleasurable recollections, and there are many in the soldier's life. Hardships suffered were remembered only to revive my hatred of the enemy who had caused them.

I secretly longed again to be in arms, and finally joined company H, second Massachusetts heavy artillery, upon its original formation at Readville. It is not my purpose to give the common experiences of the field, and therefore I omit the months that followed.

April, 1864, found at Plymouth, N. C., two companies, H and G, of the second Massachusetts heavy artillery, garrisoning the forts and redoubts on the hostile borders of a rebellious State. Plymouth is situated on the Roanoke River, at the head of the Albemarle Sound. This post was commanded by Brigadier-General Wessels, whose brigade consisted, besides the two companies mentioned, of the following regiments: sixteenth Connecticut, one hundred and first Pennsylvania, eighty-fifth New York, a New York independent battery, twenty men of the twelfth New York cavalry, a few negro recruits, and two companies of loyal North Carolinians. Upon our arrival (which was in February, 1864), we found the place in what a wag of our company termed a dilapidated condition. It was the mere remnant of what had once been quite a thriving village. The rebel forces and our own had had each a turn at attempting to burn it, and thus the best built portion of the town had been consumed. At the time mentioned, the town consisted of a few tumble-down houses that had escaped the flames, two or three brick stores and houses, and the rest a medley of negro shanties, made of staves split from pitch-pine logs, in which the surrounding country abounded, and a number of rude frame buildings, made for government use, from material sawed at the steam mill which government possessed by confiscation.

The place was a general rendezvous for fugitive negroes, who came into our lines by families, while escaping from conscription or persecution, and for rebel deserters, who had become lean, hungry, ragged, and dissatisfied with fighting against the Union. Schools had been established for the young and middle-aged colored population, under the able tuition of Mrs. and Miss Freeman, of Milford, Mass. The whole place had a Rip Van Winkle look, as though it had composed itself into a long sleep to awake after the era of revolution and rebellion had passed. The forts protecting this place were five in number. Extending along a line of two miles were Fort Williams, covering the centre of the town, Battery Worth, commanding the river above, Compher and Coneby redoubts, commanding the approaches of the left; while on the right, standing out half a mile, unconnected with those described, was Fort Wessels. Still farther to the right was Fort Gray, standing alone, one mile and a half up the river, on what is known as "War Neck," having no communication with the works described except by a foot-bridge consisting of single logs laid across a swamp, or by a boat on the river. A little tug-boat, called the Dolly, was continually plying between Fort Gray and the town. A line of rifle-pits connected Fort Williams, Coneby and Compher redoubts, with Battery Worth.

On the morning of April 17, 1864, the consolidated morning report to the adjutant-general gave eighteen hundred men armed and equipped for duty. These men were to guard and defend a line of nearly three miles, where the difficulty of communication, and consequent concentration of men at the point of attack, was very great. The theory that a long line is a weak line was here exemplified. One strong bastioned work, with a good water battery connected by parallels, with strong abatis work, would, with the same number of men, have made the place much stronger, if not impregnable. On the afternoon of the 17th, while on my way to Fort Wessels, I met two drummer boys belonging to Fort Gray on their way to the commanding general, with the information that the rebels were approaching in strong force within two miles of Fort Gray. This alarm sent

me back to Fort Williams, where I arrived just as the
enemy opened fire from the edge of the surrounding
woods. That evening a battery opened on Fort Gray,
followed by two charges of the rebel infantry, in which
the rebels were repulsed with heavy losses. Thereafter,
at that point of our line, they contented themselves by
skirmishing, and an occasional shot from their artillery.

On the afternoon of the 18th, our pickets, after disputing every step of the way, were driven in, and the
rebel artillery, from their whole line in front, opened fire
upon Fort Williams and the town. We returned the
fire. The gunboats Miami and Smithfield did terrible
execution. The battle was raging fiercely, when, in
obedience to orders, I passed down through the town to
the river. The shot and shell shrieked through the
town, crushing through the walls and roofs of the
houses and shanties. On the side of the houses towards
the river were amusing groups of negro men, women,
and children, who had gathered in the rear of their frail
shanties, as if vainly hoping they might prove a protection against the iron messengers of death. They made
a preposterous noise, in which were mingled religious
exclamations, prayer and supplication, with shrieks and
lamentations.

I passed safely through the town, and getting up
steam on board the "Dolly," was fortunate enough to
get her, with rations, to Fort Gray, much in want of
supplies. A rebel battery, commanding the river, had
made it difficult and dangerous to make the attempt.

I was fortunate in escaping the attention of the rebel battery, and arrived with the dead from Fort Gray. That night Sergeant Evans and myself buried the dead we had brought down. The rebels had been repulsed all along the line, with the exception of Fort Wessels, which, with a garrison of eighty men, had twice repulsed the rebels, and had taken thirty prisoners, but at last had surrendered to overwhelming numbers, not, however, until a rebel battery had been planted less than a hundred yards from them.

After the fight I visited my old quarters, but found them knocked to pieces by shell and shot. I extricated from the ruins two blankets, in which I rolled myself, to sleep. This was about two o'clock in the morning. In about an hour I was aroused by hearing a heavy firing in the direction of Fort Gray. Rumors came that a rebel ram was coming down the river. Without firing a shot, — throwing from her smoke-stack huge volumes of pitch-pine smoke, — she passed within a few rods of Battery Worth, commanded by Lieutenant Hoppin, who was ordered, some five minutes before she hove in sight, to fire on the first thing coming down the river, as it would be the rebel ram. At this battery was mounted a rifled gun, carrying a chilled end shot, weighing two hundred pounds, — enough, one would think, to blow the ram into the swamp on the opposite side of the river. Yet not a shot was fired from this gun until after she had passed below her, and sunk the Smith-field, whose crew were killed, captured, or drowned, while the Miami ran away. Captain Flusher, commanding the gunboats, had lashed the Miami and the Smithfield together with heavy chains, hoping in this way to detain the ram and sink her. While endeavoring to throw a shell down the smoke-stack of the ram he was killed.

From the time the rebel ram passed our batteries, the loss of Plymouth was a foregone conclusion. During the night the rebels had thrown a pontoon bridge across the river on our left, and early the same morning they carried, by assault, our redoubts on this flank, which gave them the town in our rear, and soon had sharpshooters in every house, picking off our gunners. Such was our situation on the morning of the 20th. There was no fighting at Fort Gray; Fort Williams alone returned a feeble fire upon the artillery planted upon all sides of them. The outworks soon surrendered, and Fort Williams sustained the conflict alone. Though summoned to surrender, and threatened with "no quarters" if we did not comply, we fought them single-handed until afternoon, when again being summoned, and our situation such that it was useless to contend longer against overwhelming numbers, the commanding General reluctantly surrendered, and I was again a prisoner of war.

It is a pleasure to know that most of the men and officers of the second behaved with gallantry, as also did the other regiments in the field. The conduct of one woman here deserves to be mentioned, — Margaret

Leonard,—the wife of a private of Company H, second Massachusetts heavy artillery. During the battle, she was engaged making coffee for the men in a building exposed to a heavy fire. At one time a solid shot passed through the building, taking with it one of her dresses, which hung on a nail by the wall Another carried away the front legs of her cooking-stove. Yet when the fight was over, on the evening of the 19th, she had coffee for the men, and supper for the officers. She was in Fort Williams during the remainder of the fight, and subsequently went through with a long and severe imprisonment at Andersonville, Macon, and Castle Thunder, Richmond.

During the fight, we had armed and equipped for action eighteen hundred men. The rebels acknowledged, in the Petersburg papers of the 27th, the loss of seventeen hundred men, in killed and wounded, before the defences of Plymouth; thus paying very dear for their bargain, on their own showing. When we surrendered, our ammunition was gone, and our rations nearly exhausted. In the face of these facts, and with a full knowledge of them, a rebel captain boasted that had the Confederates possessed the forts, the whole Yankee nation couldn't have taken them. He probably had forgotten Vicksburg and Port Hudson. The forces at Plymouth surrendered only to overwhelming numbers.

We were marched out between two lines of rebel infantry. As we passed along, the Secesh did us the honor to swap hats with us, by taking them from our heads and substituting their own in their place. I lost my tall dress hat, which had caught the eye of a reb, on account of the ostrich plume which embellished it. I would have preferred keeping it, as it had two very ornamental bullet holes in the top, made by some complimentary rebel sharpshooters during the action. Here let me record the fact, that many of the pretended Union men and women of the town were suddenly developed into exultant Secesh, and shouted their defiance as we passed through the place after our capture, — the same who, a few days before, were glad to draw government rations, and accept of like favors.

We were marched into the open field in front of Plymouth, where we were strongly guarded for the night. Here, also, had been driven from the town, like so many cattle, the whole population of Plymouth, except those known as Secesh. Little children at the breast, — white, yellow, and black, — old women and young, were all huddled together in an open field, preparatory to — they knew not what. There were about twenty negro soldiers at Plymouth, who fled to the swamps when the capture of the place became certain; these soldiers were hunted down and killed, while those who surrendered in good faith were drawn up in line, and shot down also like dogs. Every negro found with United States equipments, or uniforms, was (we were told by the rebel guard) shot without mercy.

The Buffaloes, as the North Carolina companies were called, escaped in some cases by swimming the river before the final surrender. On those who were not thus fortunate, fell all the concentrated rage and hatred of the rebels. Many of these Buffaloes had assumed the garb and name of our dead artillerists, and in this manner, in some instances, escaped detection and death. On our way from Plymouth to Tarboro' I saw several of our North Carolina men selected out as deserters, and, without even the ceremony of a drum-head court-martial, strung up to the limb of trees by the road-side. We were closely guarded, but not, as a general thing, badly treated.

On the afternoon of the 21st we were rationed with our captured "hard-tack" and pork, formed into line, and sadly turning our faces from Plymouth, where we had left our unburied dead, were marched into the interior. On the first day we marched about fifteen miles, and on the next, without any issue of rations, to Hamilton, where we were turned into a grove while our captors awaited orders respecting our destination. At Hamilton the citizen Secesh of the surrounding country flocked to see the captured Yankees. They were mostly women, who were curious specimens of the feminine gender, — straight-skirted, without crinoline, and invariably addressing us as "you'uns Yanks." One of the unvarying inquiries among the women was, "Has you'uns Yanks got any snuff?" It was rumored that we were to be exchanged for "Hoke's Brigade." This rumor was doubtless for the purpose of keeping us quiet and cheerful, in order that we might be easy to manage.

On the 24th we left Hamilton for Tarboro', which place we reached about noon, and where we received rations of raw meal, beans, and bacon. During the day I traded my overcoat for a two-quart tin pail, which my previous prison experience told me would be as useful as anything I could possess. It came in early demand, for that night we cooked mush. Many wry faces were made at this fare, without salt; yet, for many weeks and months after, we were glad when we got enough even of that. Here, also, the people from the town and surrounding country flocked to see the captured Yanks, bringing with them articles to trade, the women more anxious for snuff than even at Hamilton. Some of them were quite well dressed; but the majority were uncrinolined, and had a withered look of premature age, noticeable among the middle-aged and young women at the South; induced, I have no doubt, by the disgusting habit so prevalent there of "dipping," as it is called. This is performed by dipping the chewed end of a stick in snuff, and rubbing it among their teeth and gums. This habit may be accounted for from the fact that they have no useful pursuits to occupy their minds.

Most of the men taken at Plymouth were well-dressed and good-looking, and I overheard one of the young rebel ladies (?) say that she thought some of the Yanks were real "pootey," and enthusiastically declared she would like to have one to keep. Whether she meant to have one as a plaything and pet, or to keep as negroes are

kept, I know not. But the keeping, I think, by power
of attraction, would have been difficult, so destitute of
charms of person and conversation were most of the Secesh damsels there congregated. One of the sixteenth
Connecticut regiment, having a brass chain in imitation
of gold dollars linked together, traded it off as genuine,
realizing a hatful of Confederate scrip. The women
traded with us for biscuits of hoe-cake and corn, at
exorbitant prices, all anxious to get greenbacks in return, and generally seeming to shun their own currency,
especially the bills of their beloved Confederacy. They
were willing to converse, if they were allowed to do
all the talking; but were very indignant at some of
our boys, who persisted in calling their would-be nation
the Corn-fed-racy. All this dicker and talk and chaff
was carried on over the guard line. I traded off my
boots for shoes at this place, and got ten dollars "to
boot" in greenbacks, — all the money I had during an
imprisonment of ten months. Silver brought a big
premium. The common expression in exchange was,
"ten cents in silver, or ten dollars in Confederate
scrip;" and at that rate the silver was eagerly seized
upon.

We marched through the streets of Tarboro', which
were thronged with boys, negroes, old men, and ill-
dressed women and children. Some of the youngsters
wore rejected Confederate forage caps, of C. S. A.
make, much too big for them; yet they seemed to consider them a military covering, which, on that occasion,

did them honor. Passing the post-office, one of our men asked, jokingly, for a letter. The savage reply was, that they had nothing but bullets for Yankees. Arriving at the depot, we were crammed into filthy box-cars, while heavy guards were stationed on top and at the entrance of the cars. Thus packed, sixty and seventy to a car, we started, at a slow rate, forward to our destination, the engine throwing out dense volumes of pitch-pine smoke, making our journey rather uncomfortable. At noon we halted, to cook by the wayside, and again my little pail came into requisition; for, after using it myself, it was lent to several other parties, who cooked their mush in it. A great many were without cooking utensils; and having drawn nothing but raw rations, were forced to go hungry, borrow, or eat their Indian meal raw. Hunger will soon reduce one even to that expedient, in order to satisfy its demands.

We observed, while off the train, at different points along the route, that the track was much worn, occasionally replaced by rails of English manufacture. The guard, doubtless acting under instructions, kept alive the hopes of speedy exchange by relating fictitious conversations, which they pretended to have overheard among the officers. This was well calculated to deceive the majority, but it did not deceive me. I was on the lookout for a convenient chance to escape, and was soon favored with what appeared to be an "*opening*." There was a hole in the side of the car in which I was located, through which a man might possibly squeeze;

5

and a companion and myself determined, if we could get possession of the place occupied by two of our company, to try and escape during the night, while the train was in motion, by jumping from the car. With this idea we communicated our intentions to them, thinking they would be generous enough to afford an opportunity for our escape, if they did not wish to escape themselves. But upon our making them confidants of our intentions, they raised an outcry against us, and threatened to inform the guards if we did not desist. "We shall be shot by the guards if you escape," said they. One of these men repented of his folly after arriving in prison, and bitterly lamented that he had not then availed himself of the chances of that night. The general impression among our men at that time was, if they kept quiet, and did not trouble the rebels, their treatment, when we arrived in prison, would be much improved. Although I informed them of the manner in which prisoners were treated, they could not be brought to believe it was so bad after all.

So liable are men to deceive themselves with false hopes and expectations, that when the rebel guard informed them that their destination was Andersonville, a beautifully laid out camp, with luxuriant shade trees filled with birds, and a running stream, in which fish sported, they swallowed the whole story undoubtingly. So great was their confidence, that the rebels might safely have dispensed with a guard for a majority of the prisoners. Yet the vigilance of the guard was increased instead of relaxed, as we neared our destination, so that escape became impossible.

All along the route, at every stopping place, men, women, and children flocked to see us as to a show. Even in the night, the "Southern heart" was encouraged by a sight of the captured Yankees. They came with "pitch-pine torches" to catch glimpses of the detested Yanks. One talkative boy at a station one evening seemed very curious to see the Yanks, whom he had been informed had horns; but we told him we had "hauled in our horns" considerably since our capture, which accounted for their not being visible. The little fellow said they used no lights in that part of the country, except pitch-pine; they were rather smoky, he acknowledged, but they would put up with that willingly, "rather than not lick the Yankees." We had some talk with an intelligent Lieutenant at the same place, who acknowledged the worthlessness of their money, but said they were going to fight it out upon the resources of the country. The Confederacy, he said, had a year's provisions on hand, and would fight as long as their means lasted. "Well, then," said I, "you might as well give up your cause, for when your resources fail you are conquered, while the resources of the North are, if anything, more plentiful than before the war. Every man you bring into the field is taken from the producing powers of the country." At that instant the officer of the guard came up, and forbid further conversation with the "Yanks." Of course all conversations were carried on by us from the cars, where we were caged.

On our arrival at Wilmington, we were halted at the depot, and again were rationed with bacon and hard-tack, three of the latter to a man. During our half hour's stop at this place we set fire to a high stack of cotton bales near us, which slowly burned, but did not attract attention of our guard at the time. Feeling bound to do all the injury we could in an enemy's country, we were much gratified to learn, when we arrived at Charleston, South Carolina, that "a large amount of cotton had been destroyed, supposed to have been fired by malicious Yankee prisoners, who passed through the place en route for Andersonville." We crossed the river at Wilmington, on board of a ferry-boat, halted at Florence, South Carolina, the next day, and received rations of Indian meal. That night we arrived in Charleston, and were locked up in the work-house yard. Next morning received rations of three hard-tack per man, and a slice of bacon.

During the day we remained in the yard, bartering and trading with all who came to see us. I gave a man three dollars to get me some drawing paper. He returned, after a few hours, with two pages of an old ledger, one side of which had been written upon. I was rather angry at such a return, when he said, "You needn't flare up, old fellow, 'tis the best we'uns have." I subsequently was informed that it was the best I could have got had I gone for it myself. I wrote a letter, and put on it a Confederate postage stamp, to mail it for home. I was promised it should be sent, but it never was received. We got bread at this place for one dollar per loaf, United States greenbacks, but the desire to speculate on our necessities raised it to three dollars per loaf before we left the jail yard. The day was passed in talking and joking with such as came and felt disposed to talk with the Yanks.

In the afternoon we were taken out of prison and passed through the streets of Charleston, which we saw for the first time by daylight. Women and children crowded the streets, and showed us much sympathy in various ways, by acts as well as words, the women furnishing the prisoners with tobacco, cigars, and food, for which they would accept no recompense whatever; these, however, were mostly Irish or German. But through the whole of Charleston not a disrespectful or unkind word was uttered in our hearing. Sympathy with the Union cause, or possibly the constant firing down the harbor, had a beneficial effect upon the inhabitants, and in their conduct towards us. We halted on our march through the town at a German cigar manufactory, where a fine-looking, keen-eyed young German presented us with cigars and food, and a very pretty young lady made a present of a bouquet to a good looking young fellow of our number. Having some paper with me, while seated on the pavement waiting for orders I drew several hasty sketches, and presented them to the people, thus leaving my card. Knowing a few words of German, I made known my wish to escape. Quite a pleasant conversation was carried on between the prisoners and the occupants of the sidewalks and houses.

On our way to the depot, we were taken through a part of the town where the shell and shot of our guns had done comparatively little injury, yet on every side was evidence of the terrific effects of our guns. At one place was a building destitute of a corner; another had a round hole punctured through the brick walls, where the shot and shell had travelled. I guessed at the object in thus taking us through that part of the town which had suffered least, as having reference to our probable exchange at no very distant day. They wished us to get a favorable opinion of the damage done to the town by our shot and shell from the islands and marshes. We were so kindly treated at Charleston that we left the city with regret, and were again packed on board of box-cars, preparatory to leaving for Andersonville. The captain, commanding our guard while in the city, was the son of the Irish patriot (?) Mitchel. Before the cars started, an old German woman came around inquiring for me; and I have no doubt I missed a good chance of escape in being forbidden by the guard to talk with citizens.

The next day we arrived at Macon, Georgia, where we halted for a time. Macon had quite a prim, New England look, unlike any southern village I had before seen. It reminded me of Augusta, Maine.

The weather was rainy, drizzly, and suffocating on the last of our journey, and a gloom pervaded our thoughts and feelings. During the whole day, through anxiety, as we neared our destination, scarcely a word was spoken. We arrived at Andersonville about four o'clock P. M., May 1, 1864. It was raining severely when the train reached the place. Even then we did not imagine to what kind of quarters we were to be consigned. The guard answered our interrogations as to where we were going to put up, by ironically pointing out some comfortable looking barracks as our habitations.

Suddenly the whole scene changed! A ferocious, round-shouldered little man, mounted upon a bay mare, surrounded by the guard who were to take the place of those who had accompanied us on the cars, came raving, swearing, and tearing round in a most extravagant manner. So ridiculous appeared to us his gestures, person, and looks, that we burst into a roar of laughter; whereupon he turned upon us, bristling with rage, exclaiming, "By Got! you tam Yankees; you won't laugh ven you gets into the pull pen." It was a gratuitous prophecy, afterwards understood in all its horrors; and the threats of Captain Wirz had too much significance in them to be laughed at. The recollection, even now, of the light manner we received so gross a monster, causes a shudder when I think what action our laugh might have prompted him to. I was selected out, on account of my sergeant's uniform,

when, asking me if I could write, I was furnished with
paper, and told to take the names, regiment, and company of my car load of companions. When it was
done, the names of some thirty more were given me,
making in all ninety men, which was called "Detachment 21–30." The other prisoners were similarly divided, and placed under non-commissioned officers.

The new guard belonging to the station relieved the
old one, and we were marched a short distance, where
a curious-looking structure, fifteen feet high, loomed
up before us. Sentries were stationed on the top
of little platforms, scaffolded up near and at the
height of the enclosure. This was the "Stockade,"
which was to become our future quarters. It was composed of the trunks of pine trees, which were set ver-
tically into a trench, so close as to touch together, forming a close fence. In this manner about fifteen acres
were fenced in. As we halted before the headquarters of the prison, waiting, like so many drowning rats,
crouching in the rain, the guard, in answer to our questions as to what kind of a place it was inside the
stockade, replied, we would find out when we got in
there. They said prisoners tried to escape sometimes,
but the dogs always caught them. Never, to their
knowledge, had a man escaped, except one, and he was
drowned while trying to swim a pond to get clear of the
dogs. This was a crusher to the idea I had formed that
the stockade might prove a good place for an escape.

As we waited, the great gates of the prison swung

on their ponderous oaken hinges, and we were ushered
into what seemed to us Hades itself.   Strange, skeleton
men, in tattered, faded blue, — and not much of blue
either, so obscured with dirt were their habiliments, —
gathered and crowded around us; their faces were so
begrimed with pitch-pine smoke and dirt, that for a
while we could not discern whether they were negroes
or white men.   They gathered and crowded around us
to ask the news, and inquire from whence we came;
and in return we received the information that they had
mostly come from Belle Island, whence they were sent
the 1st of March.   The air of the prison seemed putrid;
offal and filth covered the ground; and the hearts,
buoyed with expectation of good quarters, sank within
them when they knew that no shelter was furnished
beyond what could be constructed of blankets or garments.   All my former experience of prison life had
not prepared me for such unmitigated misery as met me
everywhere.   Our poor fellows, who had so confidingly
believed in the humanity of rebels, were now depressed
by despondency and gloomy forebodings, destined to be
more than fulfilled.   Of those of our company who that
day entered these prison gates, not one third passed beyond them again, except to their pitiful, hastily-made,
almost begrudged graves.

CHAPTER IV.

Prison-Life in Andersonville. — Twelve Thousand Prisoners. — A
Shelter constructed. — Philosophizing in Misery. — Want of Fuel
and Shelter.— Expedients for Tents. — The Ration System. — Continued Decrease of Amount. — Modes of Cooking. — Amusement
from Misery. — "Flankers," or Thieves. — New Companions. —
A Queer Character. — Knowledge of Tunnelling acquired. — A
novel Method of Escape. — Mode of Tunnelling. — The Dead
Line. — Inhumanity and Brutality in shooting Prisoners. — Premium on such Acts. — Lack of Sanitary Regulations. — Sickness
and Death very prevalent.— Loathsome Forms of Scurvy. — A noxious Swamp, and its Effects. — Untold Misery. — Large Accession
of Prisoners. — Exposure to heavy Rains and hot Suns. — One
Thousand Three Hundred and Eighty Deaths in one Week. — Depression of Spirits, Insensibility, Insanity, and Idiocy. — Tendency
to Stoicism. — More Philosophizing. — Human Sympathies a Cause
of Sickness and Death. — Philosophy again. — Sad Cases of Death
from Starvation.

THE prison at Andersonville was situated on two hill-
sides, and through the centre ran a sluggish brook,
branch, as it was commonly termed. There were no
signs of vegetation in the pen — it had all been trampled out. Our squads were ordered to take their positions near the hill-side, on the borders, and partially in a
murky slough or swamp. This was between the brook,
or branch, on the north side, and was used by the prisoners as a "sink," until it had become pestilent with

dreadful stench. Sadly thinking of home, and its dreadful contrast here, that night we lay down in the rain and dirt, on the filthy hill-side, to endeavor to get rest. But when sleep visited us, it was with an accompaniment of horrid dreams and fancies, more than realized in the horrors of the future, and familiar now, more or less, to the whole civilized world. With burdened hearts we realized how hard was our position. The first morning after our arrival about twenty pounds of bacon and a bushel of Indian meal was given me to distribute among ninety men. We had no wood to cook with, when two of my comrades, with myself, succeeded in buying six or seven small pieces for two dollars, and soon got some johnny-cake made. At our coming into the stockade there were about ten thousand prisoners, increased to about twelve thousand by our arrival. The next day three others with myself formed a mess together; and taking two of our blankets, constructed a temporary shelter from sun and rain, and thus settled down, experiencing the common life of hunger and privations of prisoners. We soon became conversant with the ways and means of the prison. There is a certain flexibility of character in men that adapts itself with readiness to their circumstances. This adaptability to inevitable, unalterable fate, against which it is useless to strive, or where it is death to repine, softens much of the sufferings otherwise unendurable in such a life. In no position is this adaptability more fruitful of good results to its possessor than in prison. It enables the luckless prisoner to extract whatever of comfort there may be in the barren species of existence which surrounds him, and mitigates the mental torments and pains endured by those who are suddenly thrown upon their own resources, amid the acutest sufferings which squalid misery can inflict. While some pass their time in useless repinings, others set themselves resolutely at work, like Robinson Crusoe, to develop the resources of their surroundings into all the comforts they can force them to yield.

Originally the interior of the prison had been densely wooded with pitch-pine, in which that country abounds; but at the time of our arrival it had been, with the exception of two trees, entirely cut to supply the want of fuel demanded by the prisoners. The camp at that time was dependent upon the roots and stumps of the trees which had been cut down for fuel. A limited number of those who were among the first arrivals had constructed rude shelters of the branches of trees, thatched with pitch-pines to shed the rain. The common shelter was, however, constructed with blankets, old shirts, &c., while a great number had no shelter at all, or burrowed for the want of one in the ground. An aristocratic shelter, which few could indulge in, was made of two blankets pinned together with wooden pegs, stretched upon a ridgepole running across two uprights stuck into the ground, in imitation of an A tent; or two poles were tied together, with both the ends stuck into the ground, forming a semicircle. Over three of these

a blanket was stretched. A hole was then dug two
or three feet deep under the space sheltered by the
blankets. These, as a rebel surgeon one day remarked,
were little better than graves. When there was a
sudden shower, as was often the case, these holes
would as suddenly fill with water, situated as most
of them were on the side hill. All over camp men
might be seen crawling out of holes like half-drowned
kittens, wet, disconsolate, and crestfallen. Those who
could summon the philosophy to laugh at the ludicrous
view of their troubles, would find but little comfort in
such uncomfortable circumstances. These shelters were,
at best, but poor protection against rain or a tropical
sun; but, as poor as they were, many who had blankets
could not, though surrounded by woods on the exterior
of the prison, get the necessary poles or branches to
construct them. Under such circumstances the unlucky
prisoner burrowed in the earth, or laid exposed to the
fury of rain and sun, and often chilly nights and
mornings.

The organization in camp for the issue of rations
was as follows: The men were divided into squads of
ninety, over which one of their own sergeants was
placed. Over three nineties was also a chief sergeant,
who drew rations for the whole. Every twenty-four
hours these sergeants issued rations, which they drew
at the gate from the prison authorities. The sergeants
of nineties issued to sergeants of thirty or ten to suit
convenience, and facilitate the distribution of rations.

The rations were brought into camp by mule teams, driven by negroes, or, more commonly, by prisoners paroled and detailed for the purpose. A sergeant of ninety men was entitled to an extra ration for his trouble. I resigned, however, my position as sergeant of ninety before I had held it twenty-four hours, as I had foreseen that the position required a great deal of work, and I did not believe in taking an extra ration, which would not have benefited me. It was a task, however, which many among a multitude of hungry mouths were ready to take upon themselves, and but very few qualified to fill in an honorable, impartial manner. When men are cut down to very low rations, they are not always discriminating in attaching blame to the proper source, which made the place all the more difficult to fill with credit. This I early foresaw, and, therefore, left the position to some one anxious to fill it.

During the first month of our imprisonment the rations were better than at any subsequent period, except wood, of which by chance we got none. Yet even at this time the rations were miserably inadequate to anything like a healthy organization. Our rations per day, during the first month, were a little over a pint of Indian meal, partly of cob ground with the meal, which was made into mush, and which we called by the appropriate name of chicken feed. Once in two days we got about a teaspoonful of salt. At first, bacon was issued in small quantities of fifteen to twenty pounds to ninety men, but, after the first of July, this was dropped almost entirely from prison rations. Sometimes, instead of Indian meal, we got rice or beans; but each bean had had an occupant in the shape of a grub or worm. Our modes of cooking were entirely primitive. The meal was stirred into water, making a thick dough; then a little meal was sprinkled on the bottom of a plate or half of a canteen, to keep the dough from sticking. The dough was then placed in a plate or canteen, which was set up at an angle of forty-five degrees, to be cooked before a fire. When the front of the cake was "done brown," the plate was fixed upon a split stick, and held over the coals until it was baked or burned upon the bottom. Our meal was sometimes sifted through a split half of a canteen, in which holes had been punched with a sixpenny nail. But even this coarse sieve left us so little of meal for food, it was gradually abandoned as impracticable. In sheer necessity of hunger, we sacrificed quality to quantity.

It was an amusing scene, sometimes, when three or four would group together to concoct a johnny-cake. One split wood with a wedge or a jackknife, another stirred up the meal, while a third got the fire ready. The process of baking brought out the amusing features of the group. One, on his hands and knees, acted as a pair of bellows, blowing up the fire; another held, extended on a split stick, the johnny-cake, varying its position to suit the blaze or coals; while a third split sticks, and fed the fire. In this manner, at certain hours of the day, could be seen groups of men all over the stockade, with anxiety painted on their features, in pitch-pine smoke; the fireman, on his hands and knees, blowing until red in the face, tears running down, making white furrows on his smoke-begrimed features; sweating, puffing, blowing, coughing, crying, and choking with smoke, especially when, as was often the case, an unlucky gust of wind blew the smoke down the fireman's throat.

I remember, at this time, the history of one day's exertion in trying to get some food ready for my hungry stomach, which is so illustrative of the difficulty generally experienced, that I will relate it. I opened the programme one morning by getting ready to cook "mush." The wood consisted of some roots which I had "extracted" from the ground the day previous, and consequently was not very dry; so, when I was stirring the meal the fire would go out, and while I was blowing the fire the tin pail would tip over. I worked three or four hours in this way without success, when I abandoned the task on account of a rain coming up, putting the wood in my pockets and hat to keep it dry. In the afternoon it cleared away, when a comrade and myself, impelled to the same purpose by a common hunger, went to work jointly for our mush. But after nearly blowing the breath out of our bodies, and getting the fire fairly under way, the wood gave out, or, more properly, was burned out. And, while we were in pursuit of more to finish our "scald" (for, with our most sanguine hopes, we did not expect anything more than merely to scald the meal), some one passing along stumbled, and upset the ingredients of our mush, and we arrived on the spot just in season to save the pail from the hands of ruthless "flankers" — another term for thieves used among us. Ruefully we looked at the composition on the ground, and then at each other's faces, and went to bed that night sadder and hungrier than we got up, without breakfast, dinner, or supper.

The next morning, in sheer desperation through hunger, to which we had not got so thoroughly accustomed as we subsequently did, we sold some article of clothing for a johnny-cake about the size of the top of my hat, and ate it with comic voracity; and I confess, with all my hunger, I could not but laugh, the whole group was so exceedingly comical and ludicrous. One of our number, never too fat, in about a month after our capture had become a picturesque combination of skin and bones, pitch-pine smoke, and dingy blue, surmounted by an old hat, through a hole in the top of which his hair projected like an Indian plume. As he eagerly, but critically, broke piece after piece for mouthfuls, and, as he termed the process of eating, demolished it, his critical eye detected a substance foreign to johnny-cake, which, upon nearer examination, proved to be an overgrown louse, which had tragically met his fate in Indian meal. The reader will

6

query, Did this spoil your appetite? I assure such, "not a bit;" for we ate it down to the crumbs, and hungrily looked into each other's face as though some one was to blame that there was no more.

Cooking our bacon was generally performed by fixing it upon a sharp stick, and holding it over a fire; by those who were lucky enough to possess the implements, or utensils, by frying over a fire; but in a great majority of cases was eaten raw, which was also the popular way of eating fresh meat, when we got it, as it was considered a cure and preventive for scurvy. But the custom, I believe, to be more owing to the scarcity of wood, than from any sanitary provision or forethought of ours. What was prompted by necessity we made a virtue of, by seeing some good in every extreme into which we were forced by circumstances. I, for one, was always too hungry to wait for it to be cooked, especially when I had to build a fire and find wood.

A favorite dish was prepared, by taking a pint of Indian meal, mixing it in water, and the dough thus made was formed into dumplings about the size of a hen's egg. These were boiled with bits of bacon, about as big as marbles, until they floated upon the top of the soup. Thus made, the dumplings were taken out, cut open, and the soup poured on, giving us a dish which was a great luxury, although under other circumstances we would not have insulted our palates with such a concoction. Sometimes we made coffee of burned bits of bread, by boiling them in a tin cup, which was greedily drank, without sweetening or milk. This was our introduction into the living death of Andersonville, which, in spite of its comic side, had not one gleam of comfort to illuminate the misery of bondage. Sad as was the introduction during our first month's imprisonment, it afterwards became inexpressibly worse.

About this time, I became acquainted with a soldier who had been in the Confederate prison at Cahawba. He had then been a prisoner a year, and was worn down to a mere shadow, by his restless spirit and want of nourishing food. He was pointed out to me repeatedly as one who had escaped several times, and had been recaptured by bloodhounds. He introduced himself one day in a very characteristic manner. Coming along, he observed us eating, saying, "How are ye?" sat down, and looking first at one of our party and then at another, to see how far it would do to go, he gradually helped himself to johnny-cake and molasses, which we happened to have as a luxury. With great coolness he gave a relishing smack to his lips, as he used up the last of the molasses on the last piece of johnny-cake, and said, "Those 'lasses are good." He was a Kentuckian, and naturally a good deal of a fellow. Nature, at least, had stocked him well with shrewdness, impudence, and daring, — qualities not to be despised in such a place. Through him I became initiated into all the mysteries of tunnelling, and other modes of

egress from prison.   I commenced my first tunnel with
him, and was conversant with all his plans.

One day this man said to me, that about all the way
he knew of getting out the prison was to "die."   They
carry the dead out, but it is hard work for the living to
get a sight.   I did not exactly understand Billy, for I
knew he had too much of the game character to give
up in despondency; and as for dying, I had no idea he
thought seriously of such a thing as long as there was
a kick in him.   You can imagine my surprise, to see
two comrades seriously lugging poor Billy out on a
stretcher one morning, with his toes tied together, —
which was all the ceremony we had in prison in laying
out the dead.   I took a last look at poor Billy as he lay
upon the stretcher, and said, "Poor fellow!   I little
thought he would go in this way."   "He makes a very
natural corpse," said one of the boys; and sure enough,
he looked the same almost as in life, only his face was
a little dirtier if anything.   The next day I was startled
to hear, that after Billy was laid in the dead-house,
he took to his legs as lively as ever, and walked away.
He never was heard of in my prison experiences again,
and probably escaped to Sherman's army, which was
then at Marietta.

Tunnelling was performed in much the manner
woodchucks dig their holes.   First, a hole was sunk
about five feet in the ground, then were commenced
parallels, the hole sufficiently large to admit one.   The
labor was performed during the night, and the dirt

" He was shot through the lungs, and laid near the dead line
writhing in torments during most of the forenoon." — Page 85.

carried off in haversacks and bags, and scattered around camp. The mouth of the tunnel was covered up during the day to prevent discovery, which was more liable to happen than otherwise, from the fact that gre inducements of extra rations were offered to spies. I was engaged in digging, during the first month, on no less than four, which were all discovered before being finished.

One of the great instruments of death in the prison was the dead line. This line consisted of a row of stakes driven into the ground, with narrow board strips nailed down upon the top, at the distance of about fifteen feet from the stockade, on the interior side. This line was closely guarded by sentinels, stationed above on the stockade, and any person who approached it, as many unconsciously did, and as in the crowd was often unavoidable, was shot dead, with no warning whatever to admonish him that death was near. An instance of this kind came to my notice the second day I was in prison. A poor one-legged cripple placed one hand on the dead line to support him while he got his crutch, which had fallen from his feeble grasp to the ground. In this position he was shot through the lungs, and laid near the dead line writhing in torments during most of the forenoon, until at last death came to his relief. None dared approach him to relieve his sufferings through fear of the same fate. The guard loaded his musket after he had performed this dastardly act, and grinning with satisfaction, viewed the body of the dying, murdered man, for nearly an hour, with apparent pleasure, occasionally raising the gun to threaten any one who, from curiosity or pity, dared to approach the poor fellow. In a similar manner men were continually shot upon the smallest pretext, and that it was nothing but a pretext was apparent from the fact that one man approaching the dead line could have in no manner harmed the cumbersome stockade, even had he been inclined so to do, and a hundred men could not, with their united strength, have forced it. Frequently the guard fired indiscriminately into a crowd. On one occasion I saw a man wounded and another killed; one was lying under his blanket asleep, the other standing some distance from the dead line.

A key to this murderous, inhuman practice was to be found in a standing order at rebel headquarters, that "any sentinel killing a Federal soldier, approaching the dead line, shall receive a furlough of sixty days; while for wounding one he shall receive a furlough for thirty days." This order not only offered a permium for murder, but encouraged the guard in other outrages, against which we had no defence whatever. Men innocent of any intention to infringe the prison regulations were not safe when lying in the quiet of their blankets at night. Four or five instances happened within range of my observation at Andersonville, and there were dozens of cases which I heard of, succeeding the report of guns in the stockade. Scarcely a night or day passed but the sharp crack of a rifle told of the

murder of another defenceless victim. Men becoming
tired of life committed suicide in this manner. They
had but to get under the dead line, or lean upon it, and
their fate was sealed in death.

An incident of this kind came to my knowledge in
July. A New York soldier had tried once or twice to escape, by which means he had lost his cooking utensils and
his blanket, and was obliged to endure the rain and heat
without protection, and to borrow, beg, or steal cooking implements, eat his food raw, or starve. Lying
in the rain often at night, followed by the tropical heat
of day, was torture which goaded him to desperation.
He announced his determination to die, and getting over
the dead line, was shot through the heart. One cannot be a constant witness to such scenes without being
affected by them. I doubt not he saved himself by
such a course much trouble and pain, anticipating by
only a few weeks a death he must eventually have
suffered.

Under the tortures of imprisonment, where its con-
tinuation is certain, is a man blamable in hastening or
anticipating death by a few weeks or days, thus saving
himself from the lingering tortures of death by exposure
and starvation? God in his mercy only can answer it,
and will at the final judgment day, when the prison
victim and his unrelenting foe shall be arraigned before
Him who noteth even the fall of a sparrow!

There being no sanitary regulations in camp, and
no proper medical provisions, sickness and death

were inevitable accompaniments of our imprisonment. Thousands of prisoners were so affected with scurvy, caused by want of vegetables, or of nutritious food, that their limbs were ready to drop from their bodies. I have often seen maggots scooped out by the handful from the sores of those thus afflicted. Upon the first attack of scurvy, an enervating weakness creeps over the body, which is followed by a disinclination to exercise; the legs become swollen and weak, and often the cords contract, drawing the leg out of shape; the color of the skin becomes black and blue, and retains pressure from the fingers as putty will. This is frequently followed by dropsical symptoms, swelling of the feet and legs. If the patient was subject to trouble with the throat, the scurvy would attack that part; if afflicted with or pre-disposed to any disease, there it would seize and develop, or aggravate it in the system.

In cases of this character, persons ignorant of their condition would often be trying to do something for a disease which in reality should have been treated as scurvy, and could have been prevented or cured by proper food. A common form of scurvy was in the mouth : this was the most horrible in its final results of any that afflicted the prisoners. The teeth would become loosened, the gums rot away, and swallowing the saliva thus tainted with the poison of scurvy, would produce scurvy in the bowels, which often took the form of chronic diarrhœa. Sometimes bloating of the bowels would take place, followed by terrible suffering and death. Often scurvy sores would gangrene, and maggots would crawl from the flesh, and pass from the bowels, and, under the tortures of a slow death, the body would become, in part, putrid before death. In this manner died Corporal Gibson, an old, esteemed, and pious man of my company. Two or three others also died in much the same manner. Corporal Gibson especially had his reason and senses clear, after most of his body was in a putrid condition. In other cases, persons wasted to mere skeletons by starvation and disease, unable to help themselves, died by inches the most terrible of deaths, with not a particle of medicine, or a hand lifted by those in charge of the prison for their relief.

There was a portion of the camp, forming a kind of a swamp, on the north side of the branch, as it was termed by the rebels, which ran through the centre of the camp. This swamp was used as a sink by the prisoners, and was putrid with the corruption of human offal. The stench polluted and pervaded the whole atmosphere of the prison. When the prisoner was fortunate enough to get a breath of air outside the prison, it seemed like a new development of creation, so different was it from the poisonous vapors inhaled from this cesspool with which the prison air was reeking. During the day the sun drank up the most noxious of these vapors, but in the night the terrible miasma and stench pervaded the atmosphere almost to suffocation.

In the month of July, it became apparent that, unless something was done to abate the nuisance, the whole camp would be swept away by some terrible disease engendered by it. Impelled by apprehensions for the safety of themselves and the troops stationed around the camp, on guard, the rebel authorities of the prison furnished the necessary implements to the prisoners, who filled about half an acre of the worst of the sink with earth excavated from the hill-side. The space thus filled in was occupied, almost to the very verge of the sink, by the prisoners, gathered here for the conveniences of the place, and for obtaining water. Men, reduced by starvation and disease, would drag themselves to this locality, to lie down and die uncared for, almost unnoticed. I have counted fifteen dead bodies in one morning near this sink, where they had died during the night. I have seen forty or fifty men in a dying condition, who, with their little remaining strength, had dragged themselves to this place for its conveniences, and, unable to get back again, were exposed in the sun, often without food, until death relieved them of the burden of life. Frequently, on passing them, some were found reduced to idiocy, and many, unable to articulate, would stretch forth their wasted hands in piteous supplication for food or water, or point to their lips, their glazed eyes presenting that staring fixedness which immediately precedes death. On some the flesh would be dropping from their bones with scurvy; in others little of humanity remained in their wasted forms but skin drawn over bones. Nothing ever before seen in a civilized country could give one an adequate idea of the physical condition to which disease, starvation, and exposure reduced these men. It was only strange that men should retain life so long as to be reduced to the skeleton condition of the great mass who died in prison.

In June prisoners from Sherman's and Grant's armies came in great numbers. After the battles of Spottsylvania and of the Wilderness, over two thousand prisoners came in at one time. Most of those who came through Richmond had their blankets taken from them, and in many instances were left with only shirt, hat, and pantaloons. These lay in groups, often wet through with rain at night, and exposed to the heat of a tropical sun daily. With such night and day were alike to be dreaded. The terrible rains of June were prolific of disease and death. It rained almost incessantly twenty-one days during the month. Those of the prisoners who were not by nature possessed of unyielding courage and iron constitutions broke down under the terrible inflictions of hunger, exposure, and mental torments. The scenes that met the eye on every side were not calculated to give hopeful tendencies to the mind distressed by physical and mental torture. Men died at so rapid a rate that one often found himself wondering and speculating when and how his turn would come; for that it must come, and that soon, seemed inevitable under the circumstances. No words can express the terrible sufferings which hunger and exposure inflicted upon the luckless inmates of Andersonville Prison. During one week there were said to have died thirteen hundred and eighty men. Death lost all its sanctity by reason of its frequent occurrence, and because of the inability of suffering men, liable at any moment to experience a like fate, to help others. To show funeral honors to the dead, or soothe the last moments of the dying, was impracticable, if not impossible. Those whose natures had not raised them superior to fate lost their good humor and gayety, and pined away in hopeless repinings; — dreaming of home, and giving way to melancholy forebodings, which could be productive of no good result. Others, of an opposite mould of character, whom nothing could daunt, still retained something of their natural gayety and humor amid all the wretchedness by which they were surrounded. To such trials were but so many incentives to surmount and overcome difficulties. If the prisoner gave way to languor and weakness, and failed to take necessary exercise, — if he did not dispose his mind to take cheerful views of his condition, and look upon the bright side of that which seemed to be but darkness and misery, — he might as well give up hope of life at once.

In prison one must adapt himself to the circumstances which threaten to crowd him out of existence, or die. He must look upon filth, dirt, innumerable vermin, and even death, with complacency, and not distress himself about that which is unavoidable, while he must never cease battling against them. No matter if he did know that his cooked beans had been shovelled from a cart in which, a few hours before, the dead had been piled up and taken away to the grave, — he couldn't afford to get disgusted and reject the sustenance on that account. He must eat the food and adapt himself and his appetite to relish the dose, which is not so difficult to a man when very hungry. There must be a general closing up of the avenues of delicacy and sensibility, and a corresponding opening of all that is cheerful and truly hopeful in one's nature. I do not mean that hope which buoys one up by unreasonable anticipations, and which, when disappointed, becomes despair. It should be a general, cheerful hopefulness, that builds no air-castles of exchange, or speedy liberation by raids, but sees hope even in the circumstances of misery, and draws comfort and consolation from the thought that things can be no worse. There must be a kind of mental "don't-care" sort of recklessness of the future, combined with doing what you can to comfort yourself now, which is, after all, the preservation of a soldier in thousands of cases. There is a kind of armor of indifference which yields to circumstances, but cannot be pentrated by them. As soon as one gives way to melancholy despondency, as thousands naturally do under such circumstances, the lease of such a man's life in prison is not worth purchasing.

The occasion of so much sickness and death was found in the causes enumerated, with the insufficiency in quantity of food, its unsuitableness in quality, and the absence of all vegetables. The heating nature of Indian meal—the cob ground with the corn, also had its effects in producing an unhealthy condition of things. During July one could scarcely step without seeing some poor victim in his last agonies. The piteous tones of entreaty, the famine-stricken look of these men, their bones in some cases worn through their flesh, were enough to excite pity and compassion in hearts of stone.

Death by starvation and exposure was preceded by a mild kind of insanity or idiocy, when the mind felt not the misery of the body, and was unable to provide for its wants. We gave water and words of sympathy to wretches who were but a few degrees worse than ourselves. But there was danger when we gave food that we might starve ourselves, while that which we furnished to another would not preserve his life. If you allowed every sick man to drink from your cup, you were liable to bring upon yourself the terrible infliction of scurvy in the mouth, which was as much to be dreaded as death. Even a gratification of your keenest human sympathies thus became the potent cause of self-destruction and suffering to him who indulged in so great a luxury.

The terrible truth was, that in prison one could not attempt to relieve the misery of others more miserable than himself, without placing himself in greater peril. Was it wonderful that the cries of dying, famished men were unheeded by those who were battling with fate to preserve their own lives? If there were some who turned ears of deafness to distressed tones of entreaty, who forgot the example of the "good Samaritan" in their own distress, the fault and sin (if sin or fault there was under such torture and condition) were surely not upon their own heads, but upon the heads of those who had crowded into our daily existence so much of misery as to leave no room for the gratification of kindly sympathies, and had drowned out the finer sensibilities in the struggles with despair and death for self-preservation. Subjects of pity rather than of blame, they were not allowed the luxury of pity and sympathetic action. Yet many there were, surrounded by and suffering acutest torture, who moved like angels of mercy among suffering companions stricken by famine and disease.

It is a terrible thing to feel one's self starving; to brace every nerve against the approach of death, and summon to the aid of the body all its selfishness: yet men, in spite of the necessity of so doing in order to preserve life, assisted and soothed one another in hours of sickness, distress, and melancholy; and such had a reward in the consciousness of duty performed, of unselfish devotion, surrounded by famine and death — the bitter cup of misery pressed to their own lips, yet having still a care for others, under circumstances of trial when the thoughts of most men were turned upon themselves, and oblivious to others' woes amid their own misery.

Most prisoners, being only soldiers temporarily, have at variance two distinct elements of feeling, one springing from their habitual and the other from their temporary mode of life ; one springing from peaceful associations, with the seclusions of home, or the luxury of the business activity of city life; the other from the more recent influences of the camp and battle-field. These incongruous elements are in constant antagonism. One moment it is the soldier, improvident and careless of the future, reckless of the present, laughing at discomforts and privations, and merry in the midst of intense suffering. Then it is the quiet citizen, complaining of misfortune, sighing for home and its dear ones, dreaming of seclusion and peace, yielding to despondency and sorrow. And this is perhaps fortunate, for at least there is less danger that the prisoner shall become improvident with the one element, or a miser dead to every feeling with the other. Most prisoners, in such misfortunes, are apt to indulge in a kind of post-mortem examination of their previous life, to dissect that portion of their past history which is seldom anatomized without arriving at the conclusion that present misfortunes are nearly in all cases due to some radical error in their own lives. Misfortunes render some men reckless ; others, on the contrary, become cautious through failure and wise through misfortune. And such, retracing in their leisure hours their paths of life, question the sorrowful spectres of perished hopes which haunt the crowded graveyards of the past. They draw

from the past nought but cold realities; they cut into
the body of their blighted life and hopes, and seek to
learn of what disease it died.   This is rational; it is
instructive and courageous; but, unfortunately, it is not
pleasant.   Better to light anew the corpse of the dead
past, to inwreathe the torn hair with blossoms, to tinge
the livid cheek with the purple flush of health, to en-
kindle the glazed eyes with eloquent lustre, to breathe
into the pallid lips the wonted echoes of a familiar voice,
which may discourse to us pleasantly of long departed
joys and of old happy hours.   There is a piteous consolation in it, like the mournful solace of those who,
having lost some being near and dear to them, plant
the dear grave with flowers.   It is this inward self which
is all his own that the prison leisure leads the speculative
captive daily to analyze.   After a voyage of memory
over the ocean of the past, he returns to the sad present
with a better heart, and endeavors, from the newly-
kindled stars which have arisen above the vapory horizon of his prison life, to cast the horoscope of a wiser
future.

I have spoken of a mild kind of insanity which precedes death caused by starvation and brooding melancholy, in which the mind wanders from real to imaginary
scenes.   Private Peter Dunu, of my company, was an
instance of this kind.   At an early date of his imprisonment he lost his tin cup, which was with him, as
commonly was the case throughout the prison, the only
cooking implement.   His blanket was also lost, and he

7

was left destitute of all shelter and of every comfort except that which was furnished him by companions who were sufferers in common with himself, and not overstocked with necessaries and comforts. Gradually, as he wasted away, his mind wandered, and in imagination he was the possessor of those luxuries which the imagination will fasten upon when the body feels the keenest pangs of hunger. With simple sincerity he would frequently speak of some luxury which he imagined he had partaken of. Suddenly a gleam of intelligence would overspread his face; he would speak of the prison, and say, "This is a dreadful place for the boys — isn't it? I don't enjoy myself when I have anything good to eat, there are so many around me who look hungry." And then, gazing in my face, said, in the saddest modulations I ever heard in human voice, "You look hungry too, Sarg." And then, sinking his voice to a whisper, added, "O dear! I'm hungry myself, a good deal." Poor, poor Peter! he soon died a lingering death from the effects of starvation and exposure. In the lucid moments that preceded death, he said, as I stood over his poor famine-pinched form, "I'm dreadful cold and hungry, Sarg." He again relapsed into a state of wandering, with the names of "Mary" and "Mother" on his lips; and the last faint action of life, when he could no longer speak, was to point his finger to his pallid, gasping lips, in mute entreaty for food!

Charles E. Bent was a drummer in my company, a

fine lad, with as big a heart in his small body as ever throbbed in the breast of a man. He was a silent boy, who rarely manifested any outward emotion, and spoke but seldom, but, as his comrades expressed it, "kept up a thinking." I observed nothing unusual in his conduct or manner to denote insanity, until one afternoon, about sundown, one of his comrades noticed the absence of a ring commonly worn upon his hand, and inquired where it was. "When I was out just now," he said, "my sister came and took it, and gave it to an angel." The next day, as the sun went down, its last rays lingered, it seemed to me, caressingly upon the dear, pallid face of the dead boy. His pain and sorrow were ended, and heartless men no longer could torture him with hunger and cruelty.

But while the minds of many became unsettled with idiocy or insanity, there were other instances where a vivid consciousness and clearness of mental vision were retained to the very verge of that country "from whence no traveller returns."

C. H. A. Moore was a drummer in my company — the only son of a widowed mother: all the wealth of maternal affection had been fondly lavished upon him. In him all her hopes were centred, and it was with great reluctance that she finally agreed to his enlistment. A soldier's life, to one thus reared, is at best hard; but to plunge one so young and unaccustomed even to the rudiments of hardships into the unparalleled miseries of Andersonville, seemed cruelty inexpressible. He was just convalescent from a typhoid fever when captured. In prison he gradually wasted away until he died. The day previous to his death I saw and conversed with him, tried to encourage and cheer him; but a look of premature age had settled over his youthful face, which bore but little semblance to the bright, expressive look he wore when he enlisted. He was perfectly sane, and conversed with uncommon clearness and method, as though his mind had been suddenly developed by intense suffering. His face bore an unchanged, listless expression, which, I have noticed in prison, betokened the loss of hope. He spoke of home and of his mother, but his words were all in the same key, monotonous and weary, with a stony, unmoved expression of countenance. On a face so young I never saw such indescribable hopelessness. It was despair petrified! And when I think of it, even now, it pierces me to the heart. His was a lingering death by starvation and exposure, with no relief from unmitigated misery. It seems to me that God's everlasting curse must surely rest upon those who thus knowingly allowed hundreds of innocent young lives to be blotted out of existence by cruelties unheard of before in the annals of civilized warfare. It seems to me that in the future the South, who abetted so great a crime against civilization and humanity, against Christianity and even decency, must stand condemned by the public opinion of the world, until she has done "works meet for repentance."

CHAPTER V

THE prison had a vocabulary of words peculiarly
its own, which, if not new in themselves, were
novel in their significance. A thief, for instance, was
termed a "flanker," or a "half shave," the latter term
originating in a wholesome custom, which prevailed in
prison, of shaving the heads of those who were caught
pilfering, on one side, leaving the other untouched.
Thus they would remain sufficiently long to attract
universal attention and derision. The shaving was a
less punishment in itself than its final consequences, for
a fellow with half-shaven crown was lucky if he escaped
a beating or a ducking every hour of the day. Where

a thief had the boldness to steal in open daylight, and by a dash, grab and run, to get off with his booty, he was termed a "raider," which was considered one grade above the sneaking "flanker." The articles stolen were usually cooking utensils, or blankets, for the want of which, many a man died. Either epithet, "flanker" or "raider," hurled at a fast-retreating culprit, would insure a general turnout in the vicinity, to stop the offender. If the thief had shrewdness, and was not too closely pursued, he often assumed a careless appearance, mingled unperceived with his pursuers, and joined in the "hue and cry." Woe to him who attracted suspicion by undue haste when such a cry was raised; for although his errand might be one of necessity or mercy, he was sure to be hurt before it was ascertained that he was not the offending person, and his only consolation was in the fact of his innocence, or the thought that his head, if some sorer, was wiser than before.

Scenes of violence were continually enacted in the prison. Murders that thrilled the blood with horror were at one time of frequent occurrence, — of which we shall speak more particularly in coming pages, — perpetrated by bands of desperadoes who jumped Uncle Sam's bounties before they were retained in the firm grasp of military vigilance, and, when fairly caught, rather than fight were taken prisoners voluntarily. Not an hour of the day passed without some terrible fight — often over trivial matters — taking place in the stock-

ade. The reasons which provoked fights were not often
plain; but one fact was ever apparent, viz., that hunger and privation did not sweeten sour tempers, or
render the common disposition at all lamb-like. A
piece of poor corn-bread, picked up in the dirt, a little
Indian meal, or a meatless bone, which a dog or pig of
New England extraction would turn up his nose at,
would provoke violent discussions as to ownership,
in which muscle, rather than equity, settled facts. Some
of these personal encounters ended in a general fight,
where all who were desirous of that kind of recreation
took a part. It was quite a curious fact that when
rations were scarcest in prison, fights were plentiest.
In the absence of food, some took pleasure in beating
each other. "I've not had anything to eat to-day,
and would like to lick some varmint as has," said
Kentucky Joe, a gaunt, half-starved, but never de-
sponding fellow. "I'm your man," said Pat B., and
at it they went, till Kentucky was beaten to his satisfaction, and acknowledged that "a 'varmint' who had
eaten corn-dodger for breakfast was 'too much' for one
'as hadn't.'" The writer, seeing no fun in a muss,
kept out of them, foreseeing misery enough, without
a broken head to nurse. The great mass could ill
afford to expend strength in such encounters, and it was
usually easy to keep out of them without sneaking.

I have often, however, seen men who were weak with
disease, and weak to such a degree that they could
scarcely stand, engage in pugilistic encounters piteous

to contemplate. I call to memory two almost skeleton men, whom I once saw engaged in fighting for the possession of a few pine knots! Bareheaded, in a broiling sun, barefooted, their clothes in tatters, they bit and scratched, and rolled in the dirt together. I left them, their hands clutched in each other's hair, — with barely remaining strength to rally a kick, — gazing into each other's eyes with the leaden, lustreless glare of famine stamped there — a look which I cannot describe, but which some comrade of misery will recognize.

The strong often tyrannized over the weak, and as we see it in all gatherings of men, the strong in physical health and in possessions kept their strength, while the many weak grew weaker and weaker, until they were crowded out of life into the small space grudgingly allowed them for graves. Each man stood or fell on merits different from those which had been valued by friends at home. He found himself measured by different standards of merit from those used in any of his previous walks of life. Rough native force or talent showed itself by ingenious devices for making the most of little. He who could make Indian meal and water into the most palatable form was "looked up to." He who could cook with little wood, and invent from the mud a fireplace in which to save fuel, was a genius! The producer of comforts from the squalid, crude material of life was respected as much as hunger would allow us to respect anything. He it was who got a start in the prison world, and managed to live.

It was desirable on the part of prisoners to follow some trade or occupation which should give to the individual means to purchase the few desirable luxuries which could be obtained of those who came into prison from among the rebels with permission to trade. By this method there were hopes of life, even if existence was misery. Yankee ingenuity was consequently taxed to the utmost to invent "from the rough" some kind of business that would pay — an onion, a potato, or an extra allowance of Indian meal per week. Under the fruitful maxim that "necessity is the mother of invention," it was surprising how trades and business started into life. Had these men been placed in a forest where raw material could readily be got at, I believe they would have produced every "item" of a city's wants, so well were we represented in the trades. The strivings for life were piteous, but often comical in their developments. Some traded their hats and boots, or a slyly-kept watch, for beans or flour, and with this elementary start began "sutlers' business." Another genius developed a process for converting Indian meal into beer, by souring it in water. And "sour beer," as it was termed, speedily became one of the institutions. This beer was vended around the camp by others, who pronounced it a cure for scurvy, colds, fever, gangrene, and all other ills the stockade was heir too, and they were many. You would at one part of the stockade hear a voice loudly proclaiming a cure for scurvy; you approach, and find him vending "sour beer;" — another proclaiming loudly a cure for diarrhœa; he would be selling "sour beer;" and so through a long catalogue of evils would be proclaimed their remedies.

One day I was almost crushed in a crowd who were attracted by a fellow crying aloud, "Stewed beans, with vinegar *on to um!*" The vinegar turned out to be "sour beer." Stuck upon a shingle I observed a sign which read, "Old Brewery; Bier for Sail, by the glass or bucketful, *hole sail*, retail, or no tail at all." I remember one ingenious fellow, who, with a jackknife and file and a few bits of wire, was engaged in getting into ticking order "played-out" watches, that had refused to go unless they were carried; and the ingenuity he displayed in coaxing them to tick was surprising. In one instance the watch tinker mentioned made for a friend of mine an entire watch-spring of whalebone, which set the watch ticking in such a tremendous manner, for a few minutes after being wound up, as to call forth the admiring ejaculation from the Secesh purchaser, "Gosh, how she does go it!" The watch stopped — "*rund* down," as the amazed Johnny afterwards said, "quicker nor a flash." You will readily understand that prisoners cared but little about watches except so far as they were tradable for Indian meal, hog, or hominy.

Another occupation was cooking beans and selling them by the plateful to such hungry ones as could afford to trade for them. Various were the means of "raising the wind" to obtain a supply to carry on the

trade. Often some article of clothing, or buttons off
the jacket, were traded for them. But a more common
method was to trade the buttons or clothing for tobacco,
and then trade tobacco for beans; for those addicted to
the use of the weed would frequently remark that it
was easier to go without a portion of their food, however scanty, than without their tobacco. In prison one
thus paid the penalties of bad habits previously formed.
One accustomed to the habit of taking a dram of something stimulating each day, died in prison for want of it.
Habits, like chickens, "come home to roost," and were
often the millstones that sunk their possessors into the
hopeless misery which went before death. Thus, when
only about half a pint of beans, uncooked, per day
were issued, sometimes with a little bacon, men would
lay aside a few each day to trade for tobacco.

The modes of selling were various; but the most
common way of finding purchasers by those who had
but a small capital of a few pints of beans, was to pro-
ceed to the principal thoroughfare, — for even here we
were compelled to have paths unoccupied by recumbent
men and their "traps," through a general understanding, or we should have continually trod on one
another. Broadway, as we termed it, was the scene
of most of the trading done in camp. The venders,
sitting with their legs under them, like tailors, proclaimed loudly the quantity and quality of beans or
mush they could sell for a stated price. Some would
exultantly state that theirs had pepper and salt "on to

um ; " and sometimes vinegar was cried out as one of the virtues possessed by the vender of beans, and then there would be a rush to see, if not to eat. Sometimes I have seen on Broadway from fifty to seventy venders of beans, who, together with small gamblers with sweat-boards, on which could be staked five cents, and hasty-pudding dealers and sour beer sellers, all of whom sat on the ground, looking anxious, dirty, and hungry enough to make the hardest part of their task a resisting of the temptation to eat up their stock in trade. I cannot refrain from narrating my own experience in that line, it was so characteristic of experience common to those who engaged in like speculations.

Clifton V. and myself possessed a joint capital of an old watch, mention of which has been made, and a surplus of one pair of army shoes, — for I went barefoot, disdaining to abridge the freedom of my feet when it interfered with business. We invested them in beans, which were, like those usually issued, possessed, previous to our possession, by grubs and worms. The terms of our copartnership were, that he, "Cliff," was to do the selling, while I and a companion named Damon cooked, bargained for wood, and transacted the general business of the "concern." Accordingly Cliff showed his anxious face and raised his treble voice shrilly in the market-place. The first day's sale brought us about one pint of extra beans. The next day Cliff's hunger got the better of his judgment and firm resolve to be prudent, and he ate up near half our stock in trade, which was vexatious; but I could not reprove him, seeing how cheerful it made him feel, and how sorry he said he really was. Besides, his full stomach gave him rose-colored views of the morrow's trade.

The morrow came, and Cliff made a "ten-strike," selling off all the beans I could cook, and was beside himself at the prospects of our having enough to eat "right straight along." The next morning I invested largely in beans, in all about three quarts, wet measure, and borrowed a kettle that would cook about half of them, and paid for the convenience in trade. That day proved the ruin of the bean trade. Cliff came back despondently, declaring beans didn't sell; and the mystery was soon solved by the fact that on the south side of the branch they were issuing cooked beans. Whereupon, ascertaining beyond a doubt the truth of this, Cliff and myself sat down and ate one good square meal, did the same at supper time, finished them for breakfast next morning, and lived at least one day with full stomachs — a circumstance that seldom happened before or afterwards in our prison experience. Thus ended the bean trade.

After rations were issued, there would be a general meeting of a densely packed crowd, all trying to trade for something more palatable, or for that which they had not got. Some would cry out, "Who will trade cooked beans for raw?" "Who will trade wood for beans?" "Who will trade salt for wood?" while some speculator would trade little bits of tobacco for any kind of rations. The issue of rations was often a moment of fearful excitement. A crowd of five or six thousand, like a hungry pack of wolves, would fill the space before the gateway, all scrambling to get a look at the rations, as though even the sight of food did them good. At one time, during such a scene, one of the detailed men, who acted as a teamster, — and those so employed were always men that were loudest in blaming our government and "old Abe," and were insolent and well fed, — when one of the pack of hungry wretches put his hand out to clutch a falling crumb from the cart, the teamster beat his brains out with one blow of a club. He was tried by our stockade court of justice, (?) and condemned — to cart no more bread; owing, doubtless, to the fact of his having a few greenbacks, made in selling our rations.

Among the occupations of the prison was that of baker. The ovens were made of clay, kneaded and formed into bricks. The foundation was laid with those bricks while they were in a damp condition, being allowed to dry in the sun for two or three days, and then were ready as a basis for the oven. Sand was first carefully heaped upon the centre of the foundation, in shape of the interior of it, when done; over this mould the bricks were laid, and dried until the sand making the mould would bear removal, which was carefully done by the use of sticks, at the opening which was left for a door. A fire was then built inside, after which it was ready for use. There were only a favored few who got wood enough to consummate and carry on such an undertaking. The ovens described baked very good johnny-cake, and sometimes wheat biscuit. It was a convenience to be able to get rations cooked for three or four at halves. Thus our scanty rations often had to be diminished by one half, or eaten raw. There were others who followed the trade of bucket-makers, and very fair wooden buckets were made with no other tools than twine and a jackknife. As all water, with exceptional cases of those who owned wells, had to be brought from the brook, — often quite a distance for weak men to travel in the sun, — these were very desirable. There were several kettle-makers, who found material, somehow, of sheet tin and iron from the top of rail-cars, smuggled into prison by the rebels, who were fond of Yankee greenbacks. These were also a convenience to those who formed a mess, and made a saving of wood by cooking together. These kettles were made with no other implements than a common railroad spike. They were made in the manner government camp-kettles are made, by ingeniously bending the iron together in seams, in this manner rendering them water-tight without solder. Thus Yankee ingenuity developed resources where, at first sight, there seemed nothing but barrenness and misery. I never saw a friction-match in the stockade; I doubt if there were any; yet there were always fires somewhere, — how procured I could never understand, except on the supposition that they never went out.

I have entered thus minutely upon a description of
these trades and occupations in prison, from the fact that
it explains many apparently conflicting statements made
by prisoners. While those thus engaged often got the
means of subsistence, they were the exceptions of one
to a thousand of the great mass of prisoners, who were
daily perishing for want of food and from exposure.
There was quite a sum of money circulating in camp, in
the aggregate; but eventually it got into the hands of
the Secesh, who were rabid for the possession of greenbacks. The rebels were constantly coming into the
prison to trade, having first obtained permission of
Wirz, the commandant of the "interior of the prison,"
as he was termed. They were fond of buying Yankee
boots, watches, and buttons. All superfluous things,
such as good caps, boots, &c., were freely traded
in exchange for anything eatable, or for wood. One
fact was quite observable — that when the Johnnies came
in to trade the second time, they were sharper than they
were at their first visit. The process of cutting their
teeth was rather gradual; but after a while they would
become a match at driving a sharp bargain with the
sharpest kind of "Yanks," and prided themselves on
what they termed Yankee tricks. Buttons were in
great demand by them, especially New York and staff
buttons, for which large prices were paid, and eagerly
traded for.

On one occasion a Johnny came in to trade, who
was evidently as unsophisticated and green as the

vegetables he had for sale. He traded in the first place
for a pair of army shoes, laid them down beside him,
and while busy seeing to his "fixings," one of the boys
passed the shoes around to a companion, who straightway appeared in front, and before the Johnny had
time to think of anything else, challenged his attention
for a trade. A trade was agreed upon, and the price
paid, before the Johnny found out that though progressing in trade, he had but one pair of shoes. So, for
safety of these precious decorations, he picked them up,
and holding them in his arms, indignantly declared,
"Durned if I can trade with yourn Yanks in that sort
o' way, no how." We were, according to his exposi-
tion of the matter, "rather considerable right smart at
picking up traps what wan't thar own." He was thus
entertaining the boys with these original views, when
one of our fellows, just to clinch what had been so aptly
stated by the chivalrous representative, stepped up
behind him and cut off four staff buttons, which adorned
the rear of a long, swallow-tailed, butternut-colored,
short-waisted coat. After executing this rear move-
ment, he appeared in the crowd at the front, and
offered them for sale. The Johnny took the bait, and
traded his last vegetables for his own buttons, and
started off highly pleased; and so were the boys. On
the way out of prison our Secesh friend met a comrade, whose attention he called to the buttons, "like *um*
he had on the tail " of his coat, whereupon his comrade
looked behind, and informed him that "thar was not a

8

durned button thar," when our trading Johnny loudly declared, with a rich sprinkling of oaths, that "these yere durned Yanks had orter have their ears buttoned back and be swallowed."

An Ohio boy at one time set himself up in the provision business by altering a greenback of one dollar into one hundred. We considered it fair to take every advantage of them we could contrive, and it amused us to hear them gravely charge us with want of honesty. Says one of them one day to me, "I've hearn that yourn Yanks, down thar whar you live, make wooden pumpkin seeds, and I'll be dod rot if I don't believe I got some of um and planted, a year afore this war, for not a durned one cum'd up 'cept what the pesky hins scratched up."

CHAPTER VI.

Rations decreased, and worse in Quality. — Crowded Condition of
the Prison. — Heavy Rains and Increased Sickness. — Much Filth
and Misery. — Hunger a Demoralizer. — Plots exposed for Extra
Rations. — Difficulties of Tunnelling. — A Breath of Outside Air
and New Life. — An Escape under Pretext of getting Wood. —
Captured by Bloodhounds after a Short Flight. — Something learned
by the Adventure. — A Successful Escape believed to be possible.
— Preparations for one. — Maps and Plans made. — A New Tun-
nelling Operation from a Well. — The Tunnel a Success. — The
Outer Opening near a Rebel Camp Fire. — Escape of a Party of
Twenty. — Division into Smaller Parties. — Plans of Travel. —
Bloodhounds on the Path. — The Scent lost in the Water. — Va-
rious Adventures. — Short of Provisions. — Killing of a Heifer. —
Aided by a Negro. — Bloodhounds again. — Temporary Escape. —
Fight with the Bloodhounds. — Recapture. — Attempted Strategy.
— The Pay for Catching Prisoners. — Reception by Wirz. — Im-
provement by the Expedition. — Some of the Party never heard
from. — Notoriety by the Flight.

THE last of June the rations became less in quantity, and worse in quality; which, together with
the fact that the prison, originally intended for but ten
thousand, was now crowded with over twenty thousand
souls, with the incessant rains of the month, made
our situation anything but comfortable. During this
month it rained twenty-one days, almost without inter-
mission. This stirred up the refuse garbage and dirt

buried by those who were feeble and sick beneath the surface of the ground one or two feet. And whether at night, when we lay down, or in the morning when we sat upon our only bed and seat (the ground), it was miserably wet, dirty, and disagreeable with unpleasant odors. Neither could one get accustomed to, or be able to blunt the senses to, the existence of so much misery.

A great portion of my time from May to the last of June was spent in unavailing attempts at escape by means of tunnels. I was engaged in six, which were discovered by the prison authorities before their completion. Hunger is a great demoralizer, and there were men in prison who for an extra ration would inform the authorities of the prison of plots and plans in which they themselves were actively engaged. There, no doubt, was a struggle with hunger before it obtained mastery over them. Starve a man, and you stunt the growth of all his finer qualities, if you do not crush them out entirely. It changes the expression of his face; his mode of walking becomes loose, undecided; his intelligence is dimmed. Hunger blunts the keenest intelligence, and deadens susceptibility to wrong doing, and mere moral wrongs look small, or seem overbalanced, when placed by the side of food.

If you narrow down a man's purpose to sustaining his body — let his be a continual struggle for a foothold upon life, with uncertainty as to its results — give a man, in fact, crime with bread, on the one hand, and on the other, integrity and truth with death — the thousand recollections of the old home, with the arms of a dear mother or wife or children that once encircled his neck — all these recollections bid him live. Consequently, it was difficult to trust men with secrets which might be sold for bread. Again, an impediment existed in digging tunnels in disposing of the earth excavated, in such a manner as not to attract suspicion and consequent detection. These were the potent causes of failure in all our tunnelling plans. The authorities were continually on the lookout for any trace of tunnelling. "Py tam," said Captain Wirz to some fellow who had been detected tunnelling, "vy don't some of you Yankees get out? mine togs are getting 'ungry to pite you."

I had been engaged on so many tunnels which were failures, that I began to regard them as an unprofitable speculation, yielding no prospects of a desirable nature. In this frame of mind, I often queried if there was not some method by which a tunnel might be successfully completed, and began to look round me for the material with which to practically solve so grave a problem. One day, by much "gassing" and manœuvring, I managed to get outside the stockade, under guard, with several of my comrades, to obtain wood. This was the first time since my imprisonment that I had got a breath of the sweet air, trod upon the green grass, scented the sweet fragrance of the wood, and heard the carolling of birds. It was like a new

development of creation — some fairy land ! The
woods and verdant pastures all seemed so different
from the terrible pen in which we had been confined
for weeks, that nothing ever thrilled me with so strange
a vigor and elasticity. I cannot express my feelings
more than to say that I never had any previous ideas
of how beautiful the grass and woods were until suddenly contrasted with the terrible dearth of that dreadful
prison. My blood thrilled quick that morning to every
breath that reached me in the cool wood, and every
note of rejoicing freedom from the light-hearted birds
found responsive echoes in my heart.

The guards were not very strict, seemingly more
bent on trading with the prisoners than in preventing
them from running away. I commenced picking up
sticks, and thus gradually worked my way beyond
them. All at once I found myself out of sight of the
rebel sentinels, whom I left trading peanuts for buttons
with other prisoners. For fear some guard might yet
see me, I continued to pick sticks and bits of wood,
thinking, if they found me so employed, this would
deter them from firing at me, and lull suspicions they
naturally might have that I was trying to escape. I
looked around, and saw at a distance several of my
companions, who had taken the hint, following me,
picking sticks in the same manner. We got together,
and, without saying a word, by mutual consent, dropped
our wood, and ran like mad creatures through the woods
for several miles. That night we travelled, with the

exception of one hour, which was passed beneath a tree trying to get sleep, in the drenching rain. The next morning we were captured by bloodhounds while clinging to trees, and, more frightened at the dogs than hurt by them, were carried back to the prison, where we reluctantly took up our quarters again, after receiving a damning from the accomplished (?) "commander of the prison."

This adventure was one advantage to me. It showed me the way in which prisoners were hunted. I also learned the manner the guards were picketed on the outside of the prison, and fixed in my mind, by observation, the location of each. I got acquainted with one of the men engaged in hunting prisoners, and remarked to him that he would doubtless get a chance to hunt me again, and I would give him more of a chance "for travel and promotion," as we say to our raw recruits when enlisting them. This I said jocosely, not knowing what advantage it might prove to me in trying the same dodge again. Not long after, several of my friends tried the same method, and one was captured twenty miles from the prison while eating a hearty breakfast at a house where he was trapped. All this satisfied me that, with a few hours' start and with sufficient boldness, an escape was possible, in fact, almost certain, if unpursued by the dogs. Reflecting in this manner, I borrowed a map, which had been smuggled into prison, from which I traced on paper, previously greased in bacon fat to make it transparent and tough, a map of the portion of country needful for my project, with a scale of miles and points of the compass indicated on the same, besides possessing myself of all the information I could gather from numbers of prisoners who had from time to time been recaptured after escaping from prison. They all had their theories of throwing the dogs off the scent. One believed that red pepper rubbed upon the soles of the shoes would cause the dogs to abandon the trail; another had faith that fresh blood would have the same marvellous effect, and so on through the whole range of men who had been near successful in escaping. On one point, however, they all agreed, viz., that no dog could follow a man in the water on a log, or wading, any more than he could through the air, if flying.

While looking around in prison one day, hoping and wishing for something to "turn up" by which I might solve the grave question of escape, I observed an old well, partially dug, from ten to twelve feet from the dead line, which had been finally abandoned after digging over thirty feet without obtaining water. Here seemed an opening for several young men. And I thought the matter over until satisfied that a tunnel might be successfully completed if commenced in this well. One of my company had his "shebang" * near the well; and, as he was a trusty, enterprising fellow, I laid my plans before him, and finally we deter-

* Tent, spot, or blanket, or place of residence.

mined to go into the matter that night.   We made a
rope from an old overcoat which he possessed, and tying
it around my waist, I was lowered into the well about
seven feet, not without misgivings that I might travel
the other twenty-five quicker than was good for my
health, by the catastrophe of the rope's breaking, — for
shoddy is doubtful material, — or its slipping from the
weak grasp of my confederate.   I scooped with a half
canteen a place big enough to sit in.   The next day
my comrade borrowed a rope, for the alleged purpose
of digging the well deeper; and that night we dug in
earnest, and made full eight feet.   As daylight came
on, we stopped up the mouth of the tunnel with sticks
and mud, in such a manner that any one looking into
the well would not mistrust that there was a tunnel
being dug therein.   Gradually we increased our numbers until we had twenty men at work, all of whom we
knew could be trusted, as they belonged mostly to our
battalion.   We organized four reliefs, each of which
were to dig in the tunnel two hours during the night.
This made eight hours' good labor, which, considering
that we could not commence very early at night, or
continue very late in the morning, for fear of discovery,
was doing well.   The dirt excavated during the night
was tumbled into the well, and the next day we were
engaged, apparently, with the innocent task of digging
for water, — an almost hopeless task, — when in reality
our sole intentions were to keep the well from filling
up with the dirt excavated from the tunnel during the

night, without exciting suspicion.   Many a time we
were joked while engaged digging out the well, on
tunnelling "through to China," the perpetrator of
the joke little suspecting that we really were tunnelling.

Finally, after almost incredible labor, for men in our
half-starved condition, we had got a tunnel ready to
open, nearly fifty feet long, extending near thirty feet
beyond the stockade, and dug with the rude implements
we had at hand, consisting principally of half canteens
and tin quart measures, such as every soldier carries
with him to cook his coffee in.   By means of our rope,
one by one, on a dark, rainy night, we got into the well
and swung into the tunnel, one ahead of the other, on
our hands and knees, as if to play leap-frog.   We then
commenced to open the tunnel, which was rather a delicate job.   We were about six feet from the surface
of the ground, and digging up into the open air at
the further extremity of the tunnel was termed "opening the tunnel."   This had to be performed with great
care, first, for fear of being discovered, and second,
there was danger of being smothered by the falling
earth.   I had heard of one case where a tunnel was
opened in the middle of a picket fire; but it was told
that the tunnellers, nothing daunted, sprang out through
the fire; the guard, believing their patron, the devil,
had come to visit his Confederacy, ran away, leaving the
prisoners to escape.   We were not ambitious to "pass
through the fire" in any such way, and were anxious

only "to be let alone." We opened our tunnel after two hours or more of careful labor; and I, by virtue of having commenced the tunnel, had the privilege of sticking my head into the outer air first, and was not much pleased to see, sitting crouching in the rain, not a dozen paces from our opening, an outer picket guard, at a large fire. Had he not been so intent on keeping comfortable, he must have seen us, as we, one by one, crawled stealthily into the thicket near at hand. Once, when a twig broke, he made a motion to look up, and I thought we were "gone up;" but he merely stirred his fire, and resumed again his crouching position. As the last man came out, and, at a safe distance, we stood in whispered consultation, the hourly cry of the guard, "Twelve o'clock, and all is well," went round the stockade. We separated into parties of five, each to go in different directions, and, silently grasping each parting comrade's hand, we plunged into the gloomy pine forest, to make one effort for freedom.

I had fully considered for weeks all the difficulties of an escape. I would not venture going down the Flint River to the Gulf on account of the river's being picketed, and, besides, from the fact that there were several large fortified places to pass on such a route. Again, when we arrived at the Gulf, what were the prospects of falling in with any of our forces? After considering all the different points where I might reach our lines, I concluded there were less difficulties in the way of reaching Sherman's forces at Marietta than any other : the circuitous travel of one hundred and twenty miles, under favorable circumstances, would carry us through. The course I had marked out was very simple. If I tried to reach Sherman on the east side of Macon, flanking towards the sea-shore, I had many large places to pass, and such a course would throw us in contact with the many marauding forage parties which would naturally frequent that portion of the country. My plan was to go to the westward of Macon, in a north-westerly course, until the Chattahoochie River was reached, then following due north until the blue hills around Marietta could be seen, trust to fate and Sherman for deliverance.

These plans I had stated briefly to my comrades, who had adopted them, and looked upon me as a Moses, who was to lead them to the promised land. Travelling through the woods during the night, one of my four comrades got separated from the party. The next morning we reached overflowed portions of country, which indicated that we were near the Flint River. While debating as to the best course to pursue, one of my party declared he heard the hounds, which we soon found was an unpleasant fact. Not a moment was to be lost, and wading and swimming with almost frantic exertion soon brought us to the Flint River, the current of which, much swollen by freshets, was running swiftly. Getting upon logs, we floated with the stream for several hours, until we thought it sufficient to baffle the dogs from further pursuit. It was nearly noon,

when, wet and exhausted, chilled with being so long
in the water, we crawled upon the opposite shore, and
were glad to run to get up a little warmth. As we
emerged from the water, we found a sensation in the
shape of an alligator, who lay just below us, like our
floating logs.

That day we travelled incessantly through swamps,
and woods, and water, which overflowed all the low
portions of country. The only food which we had between us was a "pone" of johnny-cake, which we had
starved ourselves to save in the prison. We had a
pocket compass, which was intrusted to me, a small
quantity of salt, and a butcher-knife, such as was issued
to Massachusetts soldiers at Readville. Night came
upon us, dark and rainy, and found us still travelling
through the dark forest and wet swamps of the country. About twelve o'clock, seeing a bright illumina-
tion, which looked like a picket or a camp fire, just to
the right, about a quarter of a mile from us, we went
upon higher land to get an observation, and sat down
on some fallen logs to consult in whispers as to what
we had better do, about reconnoitring the light. Just
then I was certain I heard something move in the log
on which I sat. I sprang to my feet, with my club
poised to strike — perhaps it was a bear. I challenged
the log with the common expression among soldiers,
"Are you Fed or Reb?" "Yankee," came the reply;
and emerging from the log, which for the first time I
observed was hollow, came a human form, which, after

shaking itself like a water spaniel, asked, in tones strangely familiar, "Well, boys, what next?" "Going to tie your hands, old fellow," said I, "until daylight shows enough of you to see if you look honest." "Well, well!" laughed our mysterious prisoner; "why, don't you know Tonkinson?" and sure enough it was our missing comrade. He had escaped the hounds like ourselves, by floating down the Flint River, and by a singular coincidence had fallen in with us again in the manner related: the hollow log he had selected for his hotel for the night. As he was a sharp fellow, and had a watch, he was quite a valuable addition to our party. When this surprise was well over, we held once more a consultation about the fire which had attracted our attention, before the incident narrated occurred. We concluded the safest and best way was to reconnoitre, in order to ascertain the nature of our neighbors, and see if danger was threatening us. We found it a camp fire near a tent, at which sat a solitary picket with his gun; it was on a cross-road, stationed, I suppose, to intercept prisoners. One of our number got near enough to have knocked him over, had it been desirable. At another time that night we heard voices behind us, but concluded it was some picket tent, of which there were many scattered over that part of the country.

About three o'clock that morning it stopped raining, and we lay down together under a tree, to get such rest as we best could. It was such lodging as we were accustomed to, and the three middle ones had some hopes of keeping warm. At daylight, stiff, and more weary than when we lay down, we resumed our journey through the wood. Our johnny-cake was eaten, and during the day we stopped only to pick a few berries, which grew in the woods. We got nothing else to eat during that day. Next day, about noon, we came upon some cattle browsing in the woods. We killed a little yearling heifer, one holding her by her horns while the other cut her throat with our sheath-knife. We cut the meat such as we desired and divided it among ourselves. The skin we cut into strips, with which, and with some of our clothes, we constructed rude haversacks, in which to carry our meat. We had no matches, or other method of kindling a fire, and of course ate our meat raw, with what little salt we had to season it.

Thus, day by day, we travelled incessantly, keeping away from the white men of the country, but receiving help and direction from the negroes. Our first confidence in negro aid was not brought about by any preconceived ideas, but by accident. We discovered it was possible to trust them, to some extent, from the following incident. One day we came accidentally upon some negroes working in the woods. We ran away quickly, thinking to get out of a bad scrape. One of them called after us, saying, "Don't be afraid, massa white man." Some idea that they might give us something to eat caused me to turn back. I advanced cautiously, and speaking to an old, white-headed negro, I said, "Uncle, I suppose you know what kind of fellows we are." "Well, I reckon," he replied, rolling up the whites of his eyes. "We are hungry, and want something to eat sadly." "Well," said uncle, "you does look mighty kind o' lean. Step into de bushes while I peers round to see if we've got some hoe-cake;" and off he trotted. We kept a good lookout to see that he did not betray us. But he came back with three pones, which he "'clared to goodness" was "half they all had for de day." It was "right smart hard times in dem diggins." "Well, uncle," said I, "I suppose you know that Uncle Abe is coming down this way to set you all free when he gets the rebs licked." "Yes, yes," said the venerable negro, "I'se believe the day of jubilee is comin'; but, 'pears to me, it's a long time; looks like it wouldn't come in my time."

Bidding him God speed, we went on our way with lighter hearts at the thought that there were friends in the midst of our enemies. Some of the old negroes we met would shame the chivalry in point of humanity and good shrewd practical sense. One of my comrades who had escaped for three or four days, before this time, told me he met a negro in the woods with a gun and dog, who told him he had lived in the swamps for several years, defying the white man. He offered to take him, provide for, and keep him all winter in his hut. He refused, thinking to be successful in getting into our lines. And I was afterwards informed by some rebel officers that there was a negro who, to escape punishment, had run away from a plantation, and had subsisted in the swamps for a long time without being captured.

We were entirely out of provisions on the eighth day of our escape, and in the morning had halted in some low land in the woods near a clearing to pick raspberries, which grew in abundance. Suddenly one of our number, noted in our travels for his quick hearing, declared the dogs were after us. According to previous agreement, when we were satisfied such was the case, we separated, each running in different directions to give the dogs all the trouble we could, as possibly by this method some might escape. Nearer and nearer the dogs came. I jumped into a little brook which ran along through the low land, which was not wide enough to amount to much, as my clothes brushed the bushes on either side. But something must be done, and that quickly. Seeing ahead of me a live oak, whose branches overhung the brook in which I was running, I sprang and caught the ends of the extending limbs, and with more strength than I had supposed myself to possess, quickly threw myself on the branch, crawled towards the trunk, and went up near the top of the tree out of sight, and had just got my breath when a pack of the dogs, smelling the bushes, howling and yelping in a fearful manner, and snuffing the air, and two men on horses following the pack, came directly under the tree. Suddenly dogs and men started off in another direction, and I was not sorry to see them going. I sat in the tree, and heard them when they captured my comrades.

Another pack of dogs came around, and passed just to the left of my tree, and I was satisfied that my tactics had baffled them.

I had a good opportunity to observe, from my elevated position, the manner in which the horses followed the dogs. The men gave them a loose rein, and they followed the hounds, picking their way through the difficult places in the wood, and neighing in a manner which would seem to indicate that they loved the sport. The sound of the dogs grew fainter and fainter in the distance, until I was left in the tree to my own reflections undisturbed. Here I was. I had been without sufficient sleep for eight nights and days, almost continually drenched with rain. My hip was badly swollen with travelling; my feet bleeding, and clothes, by constant intercourse with brambles and cane-brake of the swamps, hung in picturesque tatters around me. Chilled, wet, and hungry, I got down from the tree paralyzed with sitting with my leg over a branch, shook myself, hopped around to get up circulation, congratulated myself warmly on being rather smarter than the rest of my crowd, and then sat down, taking out my note-book, in which I had kept a kind of a log, looked at my map, reckoned up the distance I supposed we had made per day, and the course we had been travelling, and judged myself from five to eight miles from the Chattahoochee River, near West Point, below Atlanta. Taking my course by the compass, I made a bee-line for the Chattahoochee River, which I determined should settle for-

"The next blow embodied a compliment to the whole pack, who had come yelling and snapping around me; and it laid one of them quivering just at the time the man following the dogs hove in sight." — Page 131.

ever the question between the dogs and myself.   I
afterwards ascertained that I had not varied five miles
in my calculations, which was quite a feather, I thought,
in my thinking cap.

When the dogs came upon us, it was about nine
o'clock, and when I resumed my journey, it was about
three o'clock in the afternoon.   I had not the slightest
idea but that those following the dogs had abandoned
further pursuit, and thus felt easy.   I had not gone
more than two miles before I heard the dogs on my
track, bellowing and yelling like wolves.   In vain I
looked for a convenient method to get out of this
scrape ; but the trees were pitch-pine, and had no
branches nearer than twenty feet of the ground.   In
this extremity I saw just below me a Virginia fence,
which I reached, and wrenching a stake from the fence
for a club, I drew my coat sleeve down over my left
hand, and thrust it out for the first dog which came up
to bite at.   He gave one jump at my extended hand,
and just at that time I let the stake come down upon
his ugly head in a manner which made him give one
prolonged yell, and rub his head among the leaves in a
way which seemed to take his mind from the business
in hand.   The next blow embodied a compliment to
the whole pack, who had come yelling and snapping
around me ; and it laid one of them quivering just at
the time the man following the dogs hove in sight, and
sung out at the top of his voice, "Let go them thar
dogs, you Yank, and get off the fence."   I saw I was

cornered, yet I did not feel like being bit up just to oblige
him. So I replied by laughing at him, at the same
time keeping the dogs off by a circular motion of my
club, remarking that I should be happy to oblige him,
but couldn't see the point of letting the dogs take a bite
apiece out of my flesh. I had noticed during this time
that he had been cocking and holding towards me a
rusty revolver, which I mistrusted, by the way he acted,
was not loaded.

After some parleying, he called the dogs off, remarking, "Well, I reckon yer are kind er tuckered eout, and
I'll gin yer a little spell at breathin';" at which I po-
litely thanked him. After some conversation, in which
he confessed that he'd "worn the seat of his trousers
a'most off toting around after us," I learned from him
that the dogs were put on our track about two hours
after our escape, but, owing to the rainy weather, did
not follow very fast, and were baffled for a long time at
the Flint River, but that, by taking two packs of hounds
on opposite sides of the river, they finally regained our
trail. Not knowing we had a compass, they had been
surprised at the almost bee line we had struck in the
woods of a strange country. After repeated requests
for me to "git into the path," which I told him I had
no inclination for until rested, I finally complied.
"Wal, I'll be dod rot," said he, laughing, "you take
it as cool as though you had caught me, instead of my
catching you." He was anxious for me to go "afore"
him. I preferred, however, to walk as near him as

possible, in hopes that he might get off his guard, and I might have the pleasure of helping him from his saddle by a quick lift of his leg, and thus gain a horse to pursue my travels under more favorable circumstances. But no such chance occurred. He informed me that he smelt a "pretty big rat," and had his "eyes open tight."

I was desperate, in spite of my seeming good nature, and went on the back track with as much reluctance as would a cat dragged by the tail over a carpet. I was once almost in the act of seizing his foot, when he caught my eye, and said, "No, you don't; yer needn't try yer Yankee tricks on me." Thereafter he kept me under range of his rusty revolver, and wouldn't allow me to come within ten feet of him. We soon reached the road and rejoined our companions, who were waiting at a cross-road with their captors.

I was informed, in my travels home, that the men employed in hunting us were all men who had been detailed from their regiments for that purpose. My captor, the head hunter, told me that he had done nothing for eighteen years but hunt "niggers." For every escaping Yankee caught, he shared equally with others thirty dollars. On excursions of the kind they sometimes killed men, but that was seldom done unless they had whiskey in the crowd. He informed me that my being captured was mere accident, as he had been out to a settlement to forage for something to eat, when returning, he had run upon my trail, and followed it up. His dogs were, he said, the best trained of any in Georgia, and would follow "nothing but humans." He used me very well indeed, and during the journey back to the stockade shared with me the food he purchased, and invited me to sit with him at table. He also paid me a rather doubtful compliment by saying, "If yer wer a nigger, I wouldn't take three thousand dollars for yer."

After a long, wearisome march backward of seventy-five miles, in which we had to keep up with horses and mules, we arrived again at the stockade headquarters. "Ah, py Got! you is the tam Yankee who get away vunce before!" was the first salutation of Wirz; and then, turning to the hunter, he said, "Vell, did you make de togs pite 'im goot?" "No," was the response. "Vell, you must next time." "If I must, I will," said the hunter; and I suspect he did, for I saw several, who were recaptured after that, frightfully bitten by the dogs.

After taking my name and the detachment I belonged to in prison, he turned savagely around to me and said, "Vell, vat you tink I do mit you?" "I am in hopes," I replied, assuming the first position of a soldier, "you will put a ball and chain on, and anchor me out here somewhere where I can get fresh air." "Ah, you likes it, toes you? Sergeant, take dis man to de stockade." Back I went to my comrades, among whom my blanket and some other things left behind had almost bred a quarrel. They were quite surprised to see me, and

were glad that I brought with me a log of pitch-
pine wood, which, through the kindness of Sergeant
Smith, I was permitted to bring into the prison. On
the whole, though my clothes were torn in shreds, and
I was scratched with briers and bitten by the dogs, my
health was better generally than when I left the prison.
It was not long before I was tunnelling again, with what
result will be hereafter shown.

Of those who escaped at the same time with myself,
eight were captured the first morning after their escape,
four got away some twenty miles, while the remaining
three I have never since heard from. My unsuccessful
escape gave me one advantage in prison; it brought me
a flattering notoriety, which led to my being made a
confidant in any plans of escape formed by those who
were knowing to my adventure. I was sure to be posted
in all tunnelling going on, and therefore, in my opinion, increasing thereby my chances for successful escape.

CHAPTER VII.

Increase of Prisoners, generally destitute. — Greater Suffering from no previous Preparation. — Sad Cases of Deaths. — Rations growing worse. — Bad Cooking and Mixtures of Food. — Almost untold Misery. — Dying amid Filth and Wretchedness. — Preparing Bodies for Burial. — Horrible and Disgusting Scenes. — Increased Mortality. — Rebel Surgeons alarmed for their own Safety. — Sanitary Measures undertaken. — Soon abandoned. — Scanty Supply of Medicines. — Advantages of a Shower-bath. — Gathering up the Dead. — Strategy to get outside the Prison as Stretcher-bearers. — Betrayal by supposed Spies. — Horrors at the Prison Gate in the Distribution of Medicines. — The Sick and Dying crowded and trampled upon. — Hundreds died uncared for. — Brutality in carrying away the Dead. — The same Carts used for the Dead Bodies and in carrying Food to the Prison.

DURING July prisoners continued to come into prison at the rate of about one thousand per week. These, with few exceptions, had previously been stripped of their overcoats and blankets, and, in many instances, had neither shoes, stockings, nor jackets — nothing but shirt and pantaloons to cover their nakedness. Numbers of the inmates of the prison had been prisoners at Belle Island, and various other rebel prisons, for a year or more, and of course in that time had got no additions to their wardrobe, except such as their ingenuity could devise. It was common to see prisoners without hat, shirt, shoes, or pantaloons, their only covering being a pair of drawers. In this manner men became so burned by exposure to the sun, that their skins seemed tanned almost the color of sole-leather. The great mass who came into prison at this time had none of the advantages arising from gradual initiation, but were plunged into the depths of prison misery at once. Without the advantages of experience, with limited means of comfort, they were thrown into prison to struggle and sicken despondently, and die. Some twenty of my company died during the month. B. W. Drake, a lad about eighteen years of age, was a victim to despondency and starvation. His delicate appetite rejected the coarse, unsalted, unpalatable food of the prison. Without any particular disease, he wasted away to a mere skeleton, and finally died. Sergeant Kendal Pearson, of my company, also one of my mess, died during the month. He had been accustomed for many years to the moderate use of stimulating drinks. In prison, cut off from these, and with no proper nourishing food to take their place, he continually craved and thought of such things. In their place he would sometimes get a few red peppers, and make from them a hot drink, which seemed for a while to revive life and ambition within him; but gradually his strength grew fainter and more feeble, till he died.

In this manner they dropped off all over the prison; and one day you would see a man cooking his food, the next day he would be dead. The eighty-fifth New York, who, it will be recollected, came into prison at the same time with ourselves, was reduced in number by death over one half. Our rations continually grew worse, instead of better. For some of the last detachments formed in the prison, rice and beans were cooked, and in the change around from cooked to uncooked food, occasionally other detachments got the same; but the food thus cooked was often fearfully dirty, caused by the beans and rice never being cleaned before cooking, and from the flies which gathered on and in all descriptions of eatables at that time of the year. The rebels said that iron wire was so scarce that they could not get it to construct sieves to cleanse the rice and beans. Had they possessed a particle of ingenuity or forethought, they might have winnowed them in the wind. The simple reason seemed to be for so great admixture of dirt, that they neither cared nor thought the matter worth looking after.

The whole prison was now a scene of misery which words cannot express, and which never was before, or ever again will be seen. At night you are awakened, your companion and friend dying by your side, his last words of pathetic entreaty for food. "Don't tell mother how I died," said a dying comrade to me; "it would break her heart to know what I had suffered. I am glad she cannot see how dreadful I look, she always loved to see me so clean." "Wash my hands and face," said another of my comrades, when he knew he must die; "I cannot bear to die dirty;" and as I washed his wan, pinched face, and browned, thin hands, he smiled, spoke the name "mother," and died. His sensitive nature had ever shrunk from the vermin, filth, and dirt of the prison, so contrary to his habits of cleanliness and gentle breeding — he was anxious once more to be clean and die. Sad death-beds were all around. On the damp, hard ground, many a mother's darling, many a father's proud hope, breathed away a life which shut the light from some household — in some heart left sad throbbings. I am glad that no mother knows all the particulars of the miserable life, that preceded death in prison. I have been questioned by many mothers, who have lost a dear boy at Andersonville. If I seemed uncommunicative, and did not desire to converse with them, and should these pages meet their eyes, let them be assured it was not because I did not sympathize with them, or that my heart was not full, but because I could not bear to pierce their hearts by detailing misery which would only bring them keener pangs of sorrow.

There comes to my vision now, sitting in the soft twilight of this evening, listening to the village church bells, the form of one who died — miserably starved — at Andersonville. When I first made his acquaintance, he was a clerk at headquarters of our commanding general. In prison our acquaintance ripened into friendship, which ended only with death. I never can forget how fond his accents were when he spoke, as he often did to me, of his village home; described the winding slopes around the river's side, where he passed on his way to school or church; and, "Sarg," said he, while his intelligent eye would fire up with softened light, in which were mingled shadows of regret, "if it should please God to deliver me out of this misery, I would try and do nearer as mother wished me." He told me how in the long winter evenings he read to her while she peeled the red-cheeked apples before a blazing fire; and then he would exclaim, "What a contrast to this scene!" Again he would look around him, and say, in those far-off, dreamy, dreary tones often heard in prison, "I wish I had the scraps she throws to our dog and chickens," or "I wish I had the straw and house our pig gets." When he died, his last, faint words were, as he placed his well-worn Bible in my hand, "I shall not be needing this, or anything to eat, much longer. I have tried to live by that book; take it — may it prove to you, as it has to me, a last solace when every earthly hope has passed away."

I opened the book, and read in low, hushed tones from Psalm xxxiv.; and when I concluded the last verse, "The Lord redeemeth the soul of his servants; and none of them that trust in Him shall be desolate," he looked up, saying nothing, but with a smile of gladness, as though that trusting spirit was his. Shortly after he became delirious, and died that afternoon — one more victim to Andersonville.

The common mode of preparing bodies for the grave was by tying their two large toes together, and folding their hands one over the other. If the deceased had a hat, not needed by others, — which was seldom the case, — it was placed upon his face; otherwise the shrivelled checks, the unclosed eyes, and drooping jaw, as they were carried through the prison, presented a pitiable sight, which I will not enlarge upon.

It was when death became common as life; when the prison, reeking with deathly vapors, was crowded to suffocation with living victims; when, side by side with life, death walked with the prisoner, — it was then that inhumanity shuddered at its own cruel malice. Even rebel surgeons, accustomed to seeing all our sufferings, protested at last, and uttered complaints to the authorities, which will bear out all the statements ever made of Andersonville suffering. Under the influence of protests from various rebel sources, men were set at work to enlarge the stockade, and again an effort was made to fill in the cesspools of the prison; but these efforts to relieve our pitiful condition never seemed to be made in earnest, but were rather the result of fear that disease would spread into their own ranks outside the prison. These efforts, too, were soon abandoned, and matters relapsed into their old condition, growing worse and worse. "If Yellow Jack gets into this here place," said the rebel quartermaster to some of us, "it won't leave a grease spot on yer; and I can't say there'll be many left if he don't."

Medicines were issued in scanty quantities for a while, in July and August, but they seemed generally a played-out commodity in the Southern Confederacy. They were variously crude in kind, and small in quantity. Bloodroot was used as an astringent; sumac berries were the only acid given for scurvy; blackberry root was given as a medicine for diarrhœa, and camphor pills were the standard medicine for various diseases. Personally I cared for none of these, as I ever placed but little faith in nostrums; but thousands of wretches, in hopes of prolonging life a little longer, crawled, and were carried, to the prison entrance where medicines were issued. "The best medicine, after all," remarked a rebel surgeon, one day, "for these wretches, is food;" and it was but little use to doctor starvation with herbs. But wholesome, nutritious food was more difficult to be obtained in prison than medicines, scarce as they were. I found one of the most efficacious remedies for the indescribable languor and weakness which result from insufficient food and scurvy to be cold-water shower-baths, taken morning, evening, and at noon. I usually showered myself by pouring cold water from my tin pail over my head and person while standing. Besides contributing to personal cleanliness, it had an agreeable, energizing action, without any of the depressing after effects produced by stimulating drinks. I do not think its influence in preserving life, in my case, can be much overstated. I practised daily bathing through all my imprisonment; and though sometimes the disposition induced by weakness and languor was greatly against exercise, yet I knew, from what I had seen, that

I must not give way if I hoped to live. Sometimes it seemed impossible for me to get to the "branch" to wash, and the water was often so filthy that it was not agreeable to use it even for bathing. Yet I always forced myself to creep to the brook and take a shower-bath. The effects were instantaneous, and sometimes seemed marvellous. I could always walk briskly back again up hill, and feel like a different man.

Looking back over the past, I can hardly imagine how I managed to live from day to day. Wood was so scarce that it was almost impossible to cook our food when it was issued raw, — as it was most of the time, in about half of the squads of the prison, who were supposed to have cooking apparatus. Every remaining root, where trees had been, was dug out with the rude implements of the prison. Every stump had claimants, who dug around it, and protected their rights from invasions by force. This, for men in our condition, was hard and wearisome work, as our implements were mostly inadequate to the task, under favorable circumstances, for stronger men. The stump and roots, after they were dug out, were cut up into small bits of three or four inches length and one inch thickness, — sometimes in more minute pieces, — by means of a jackknife, and often with merely a piece of blade without a handle. Occasionally an axe would be smuggled into prison by some mysterious means, and its possessor became a kind of prince, who levied tax upon all the surrounding miserables who required its use.

The dead were gathered up by detachments of prisoners, and laid in rows outside the stockade. In order to get wood, there was great competition to fill the office of stretcher-bearer, as there was sometimes a chance for such to pick up wood on their return. Hence it passed into a saying, "I swapped off a dead man for some wood." A stretcher was made for carrying the sick and dead by fastening a blanket to two poles, provided for the purpose, and then rolling up the blanket on the poles until about the width of those of the ordinary construction. As I have elsewhere instanced in these pages, sometimes men feigned to be dead, and were carried out by their comrades, each of the parties deriving advantage by the operation. Another sharp practice was, for four to carry out a dead man and only two return with the stretcher, which gave two a chance for escape and wood to the remaining; thus conferring mutual benefits. Nothing of this kind could be of long duration in practice, for by some method the Johnnies soon became posted in all our dodges. It was said, I know not with how much truth, every batch of prisoners sent into the "pen" were accompanied by a spy in U. S. blue, whom the others naturally trusted as a comrade. He found out all the secrets of the squad and reported them to Wirz. This, doubtless, will account for much seeming treachery among our own men. It does not seem possible that any amount of misery could induce comrades to betray one another, even for food. I class traitors as follows: First, bounty jumpers;

second, enlisted prison convicts; third, men who dug tunnels for the purpose of discovering them to the rebels, gaining thereby an extra ration; fourth, spies sent in by the authorities.

Inside the stockade, near the gate, was often the scene of wildest horror. Here would be gathered together in the morning, waiting to pass out the gate to booths where medicines were distributed, the sick, creeping, often, upon their hands and knees, and those too sick to creep borne by feeble, staggering companions. Here, also, would be gathered the stretcher-bearers with their burdens of dead; all waiting, in a densely-packed throng of thousands, often in the rain, or sultry tropical sun, where not a breath of air stirred to revive the fainting. It was a rule, that no one, however sick, could be prescribed for or receive medicine unless first carried to the doctor. As it could never be ascertained on what day or hour medicines were given, day after day these suffering thousands would be turned away without medicines, after waiting for hours through the intense heat of the meridian sun. Often the sick, abandoned by those who carried them, would be left near the gateway, in the intense heat, where no air could reach them, and thus uncared for, die. This arose not so much from the want of feeling of comrades as from their inability to care for them. Those who bore stretchers often fell fainting, and died in that throng of waiting misery. One day, in July, twenty men died in less than four

10

hours among the crowd of dead and dying around the prison gate.

The numbers who went to the hospital outside corresponded with the numbers who died there daily. A police force of the prison dictated, with clubs, who were to pass first through the gate. The dead took the preference, followed by the sick on stretchers. Few of this throng got medicines. A great mass of the sick, rather than suffer the jamming and crowding, and rather than witness these depressing scenes of horror, remained, without trying to obtain what they came for; since, to pass through this truly horrible ordeal, to go through or stand among this crowd of dead, sick, and dying, was worse than the suffering it was intended to alleviate. I considered myself rather a tough specimen of a prisoner, but, after waiting, without success, for four successive mornings, to get out a comrade, I became confident, if I persisted, I should be "carried out with my toes tied together" (which, in prison language, meant dead). Imagine two or three thousand men struggling, suffering, crowding together, to get through the gate, — all forms of death, disease, and sickness crowded and jammed together. Here the dead were crowding and jostling against the sick, and the sick, in their turn, jostling against and overturning the dead and dying.

From first to last, the system of dispensing medicines was productive of more suffering than it relieved. At such gatherings the stench arising from the dead and dying was dreadful enough to make well men sick; while the sight of men sick and dying, under the circumstances described, was sufficient to depress the strongest heart with terror. The wan, pinched, famine-stricken, dirt-clotted countenance of the poor sufferers, the disgusting spectacle of dead men with unclosed eyes and drooping jaw, the eyes and face swarming with vermin, combined to make the scene one of the most intense horror ever gazed upon by mortal eyes. One of my battalion, a private in Company G, was carried for two successive mornings to this gathering, and on the third died, lying in the hot sun, without an effort being made by the surgeons and attendants to obtain shelter for him. Hundreds died in this uncared-for manner, which was of too frequent occurrence to be noticed or noted. One would naturally suppose such spectacles enough to excite in hardened hearts emotions of pity and remorse; but the chivalry gazed upon these daily, unmoved, often remarking upon them, "Good enough for the damned Yanks." Neither were the dead and dying exempt from their abuse. I have seen a dying man rudely tumbled from the stretcher on which he lay, without the slightest heed being given to his pleading entreaties for pity.

On one of the mornings when I was carrying the sick, I saw an emaciated, sick man upon a stretcher; his shrunken face and hands were covered with filth, and begrimed with the pitch-pine smoke of the prison; he had no clothing upon his wasted body save a pair of army drawers, which had once been white; otherwise diarrhœa had rendered his condition too dreadful to be described to ears polite, or even to be gazed upon. One of the prison officers at that time crowded through the throng of the sick and the dead: while doing so, he forcibly pushed against this poor creature, who was uttering plaintive moans and cries for mercy, to which no heed was given. In the scramble which followed, the dying man was overturned, and, as he lay gasping in his last trembling agonies, the same officer or attendant passed again that way, and rudely thrust him with his foot from his path, saying, "One more Yank's gone to the devil." Sitting this evening before the crackling blaze of a New England's winter fire, and cheered by civilized comforts, I cannot repress a chill of horror and creeping sensations of shivering terror at its mere remembrance.

Such occurrences were too much a "matter of course" to be noticed, and I only instance this solitary, unknown dying man, among the suffering thousands of the prison pen, as an example of the fiendish hate and malice which pursued these patriots of the Union even when the doors of death were closed upon their starved, unburied forms!

Carrying away the dead to their final rest was but a horror in keeping with the scenes described, and a fitting climax to the life of misery which ended in the prison. The dead that gathered during the day were placed in what was known as the dead house, — a rude shed frame, covered with bushes. From thence, each morning, they were taken, thrown upon a cart drawn by three mules, with a negro driver seated upon the middle one, over the ungraded field to the place of interment. The bodies were usually thrown, one upon the other, as high as could be reached; often the head, shoulders, and arms of one or more of the bodies protruding over the side and from the rear of the cart, or from under the dead piled above them, — the dropping jaw, the swaying head, undulating with each motion of the cart, the whole mass of bodies jolting and swaying, as a comrade expressed it, "like so much soft soap." It was said that from these carts maggots and vermin of various kinds could be scooped, after such an excursion, by the handful. In these same carts our rations were brought to us, shovelled in where the dead bodies had lain; and with flies, which gather, in a climate like Georgia, upon all eatables exposed, gave us food, when cooked, well mixed with everything which could be offensive and disagreeable. Death in prison, under such circumstances, was not always looked forward to with loathing or terror, — not always preceded by acute, though always with great suffering, — but was often hailed with tearful, trembling joy, as a message of freedom spoken to imprisoned men.

CHAPTER VIII.

FROM the time we arrived in prison we were continually troubled and annoyed by having our scanty clothes, blankets, and cooking utensils stolen from us. There were so many temptations, and so few restrictions thrown in the way of the perpetration of theft, that it became an evil, at last, that must be checked. Stealing blankets from boys unaccustomed to hardships was downright murder; for, if no one extended the corner of his blanket to protect the unfortunate from the chill dews of evening and from the frequent rains, deprived thus suddenly, he was sure to sicken and die. Stealing cooking utensils reduced unfortunates, thus deprived, to the necessity often of eating their scanty rations without cooking, or of steal-

ing or begging from others. Begging was as much out
of fashion and good standing in prison as any place.

It was rumored around camp, from time to time, that
raiders and flankers were organized for the perpetration
of outrages, and of protecting themselves against the
punishment of such acts. Although there was no defi-
nite organization among us, it was agreed upon that
these villains should be promptly dealt with ; that when
any of the Plymouth prisoners could identify a "raider,"
or was attacked or robbed by one of them, he was to
call out loudly "Plymouth !" when every one of the
boys within hearing were to turn out to his assistance.
In accordance with this agreement, we heard one morning the rallying cry, and captured a fellow who was
caught in the act of stealing a blanket. The boys gathered around him, not knowing what to do with the
Tartar now that they had caught one. He sat gnashing his teeth, threatening his captors with the vengeance
of a band, which he said was formed for mutual thiev-
ing, if they should injure or inflict punishment upon
him. Feeling some reluctance to proceeding against
him, they were about to release him without punishment, otherwise than a few kicks, when a corporal of
Company G, second Massachusetts heavy artillery, fa-
miliarly known in prison as "Big Peter," came into the
crowd, and taking the raider fearlessly in hand, inflicted
summary punishment upon him by shaving half of his
head and face, giving no heed to the desperado's savage
gnashing of teeth and threats of vengeance, except to

thump his head at each beginning and repetition of them. After dealing out justice in this off-hand manner, and an administrative reminder (in the rear) from a pair of the heaviest of cowhides, the thief was released, with admonitions to sin no more.

This, I believe, was the first instance of formal punishment for such misdemeanors; and thereafter Big Pete, by virtue of these services, became the terror of evildoers. Pete exhibited so much courage at this time, and subsequently so much good sense and natural judgment, that he gradually became the administrative power for the punishment of offences committed. He performed for us the services of shaving, and in a dignified, impartial manner gave the culprit a trial, — hearing the statements of both sides before pronouncing judgment and inflicting punishment, both of which, however, were often condensed into the last act. Few exceptions were taken to his rulings, for who could object to the persuasive arguments of one who wore such heavy boots?

The incident narrated was the beginning of a power in camp to punish offenders, which finally provided us with an effective police organization. Pete was an uneducated Canadian — a man of gigantic stature and great physical strength, of an indomitable will, great good nature, and with innate ideas of justice, in the carrying out of which, he was as inflexible as iron. A blow from his fist was like that from a sledge-hammer, and from first to last he maintained so great a supremacy in camp, that no description of the prison at that time would be complete without a sketch of him. His trials were often intensely grotesque and amusing to spectators, but not generally so to the culprit. I took pains to follow some of his trials, and I must say, in justice, I never knew him to make a wrong decision, though baffled in his purpose by ingenious lies. Through all the intricate lies, he had a talent for detecting them and sifting out the truth. Thus, at last, by common consent, if any one had complaints to make, he carried them to the "shebang" of Big Peter. He either went himself, or sent some of his adherents, who returned with the accused; witnesses were then summoned and punishments dispensed. Justice was being dealt out in this manner, when one morning it was announced — and to our sorrow we found it carried into practice — that our rations were to be stopped on account of men being missing from the stockade — supposed by the rebel authorities to have escaped by means of tunnels. Investigation led to no new discoveries, and after twenty-four hours' extra starvation, they were again issued as before, it being impossible to discover the missing men, or any modes by which they could have escaped.

About this time, the raiders, under the leadership of one Mosby, became exceedingly bold, attacked new comers in open daylight, robbing them of blankets, watches, money, and other property of value. Rumors of frightful import were circulated through the camp of men murdered for their blankets and money. After this, more men were missing at the morning roll-call, of whom there could be no reasonable account given. Under Big Peter a company was organized, armed with clubs, who proceeded to the shelter formerly occupied by the missing men. Inquiries being made among those who were living near, no information could be obtained, otherwise than the fact that outcries were heard during the night, and that there was a scuffle near; but scenes of disorder being common during the night, they had taken but little notice of them, since, as peaceable men, they wished to avoid all wrangling. Nothing at first could be found, in the shelter formerly occupied by these men, to excite suspicion. Most of the crowd had dispersed, when one of the men, on his hands and knees at the entrance, looking down into the grave-like hole which formed the principal part of the abandoned dwelling-place, saw a piece of blue cloth, partially covered with dirt. Seeing in this the element of a patch for the repairing of his shattered wardrobe, he pulled at it, and found it fastened in the ground. This excited his curiosity, also his desire for possession; and he began to dig and pull, until further progress was arrested, and he started back with horror at the unexpected appearance of a human hand. A crowd gathered around, and speedily a dead man was unearthed, whose throat had been cut in a shocking manner, and his head bruised by a terrible blow. In the same space, beneath him, was found another victim, with his throat cut. The news of these horrible murders spread through the prison, as if by telegraph, and a large crowd soon assembled around the scene of these atrocities. The police proceeded to the shelter of several notorious thieves and bad characters of the prison, and arrested them. Through information, or clew gained of one of these, they were induced to dig in the shelter of some of those arrested, which resulted in the discovery of money, watches, &c., in many cases identified as the property of the murdered men.

Rapidly after the perpetration of these cold-blooded atrocities, strong police forces were formed under Big Peter as chief of police. Afterwards a judge-ship was established in prison, and there were two regular practising attorneys, who took fees of Indian meal, beans, and small currency in payment for services rendered; and sometimes, it was said, bribed the judge and chief of police. In the case of Staunton, a big brute, and tool of the rebels, who killed a man, as mentioned in preceding pages, it was rumored that his money, procured by dicker with prisoners, obtained him a mild sentence and punishment. Not to digress further, the supposed murderers, some fifteen in number, were arrested, and after gaining sufficient evidence, consent was obtained of the prison authorities for their trial. Besides this was obtained the privilege of conducting the trial under guard, in a building outside the prison. The accused were also held in custody through the kindness of Wirz, the commandant. A jury of men was empanelled, composed of prisoners just captured, who had never been in the prison, and who, therefore, could not have formed prejudices on either side. The trial lasted through a number of weeks. Competent men were appointed to defend the prisoners by the authorities. An able lawyer, an officer of the rebel guard, conducted the defence, afterwards stating to me that he had no doubt of the guilt of those who suffered punishment. The prosecution was conducted by men selected from among the prisoners. Six of these men were pronounced by a jury guilty of murder.

On the 12th of the month, Captain Wirz, accompanied by a guard, brought the prisoners into the stockade, where, on the south side, near the gate, and the scene of the murder, a gallows had been erected. Here he turned the offenders over to the prison police, with a short speech, in which he stated that they had been impartially tried and found guilty of atrocious murders, and that he left their punishment in the hands of the prisoners of the stockade. He then turned, and followed by his guard, left the prison. The police formed, in two ranks, a hollow square around the gallows; the ropes were arranged, and the guilty men ascended the scaffold steps. Up to this time the murderers did not seem to view the proceedings in a serious light, but rather as a joke. Leave was then given for them to speak, which they did, protesting their innocence, one or two calling upon their companions to do their duty, which, properly interpreted, meant that they wished to be rescued from the police. The ropes were adjusted about their necks, the bags were drawn over their faces, their hands pinioned, a hushed silence reigned in the camp, the drop fell, and five of the prisoners hung by their necks, swaying in the air; the sixth, nearest to the prison gate, sprang at the time, or before the drop fell, broke the rope about his neck, gained his feet, forced his way through the police and crowd, cleared his hands, ran swiftly, was pursued, beaten over the head, and recaptured, when the rope was again adjusted, his protestations of innocence were unheeded, and he was pushed from the drop, and hung with his comrades in guilt. Thus ended the lesson of retribution that put a stop to murders in prison, and broke up a gang of bounty-jumping desperadoes.

Let me here record, in justice to a man who has since met a similar fate, in retribution for crimes committed against Union prisoners, that I and many others of the prison were grateful to Henry Wirz for the privilege afforded us, to enable us to give the accused a fair, impartial trial. I have purposely avoided, in these pages, heaping unnecessary odium upon the head of one who, though guilty, I have good reasons to suppose was only the executive of a system devised by men high in rebel authority, and from whose orders no inferior could deviate. There never was a hanging conducted in a more orderly manner. There was no clamor of voices, but in silence and decorum befitting such a scene, thirty thousand men were its witnesses. Thenceforward raiding and flanking were of rare occurrence, and the police became one of the establishments of the prison. That the police did much to punish offenders and preserve order, cannot be denied. They were mostly of the class denominated "roughs," selected for their physical rather than mental qualifications, and in some instances became a greater evil than that which they were instituted to correct. They levied tax upon all trading stands and occupations in the prison, cudgelled men over the head for small faults, and whipped them upon the bare back, with a cat of nine tails, most of whom, however, deserved the punishments inflicted. Yet they would not tolerate any injustice done by others than themselves, unless they were well paid for not arresting offenders. Reserving to themselves the right (?) of doing injustice and committing abuses, they governed the camp and corrected all other abuses but their own.

I am sorry to record, that in the Florence (S. C.) military prison, when S. was acting chief of police, this kind of police force became for a while degraded tools in the hands of the rebels, and whipped men at their command upon the bare back for digging tunnels, &c., for which dirty service they were rewarded with extra rations. I have entered thus particularly into details which were needful that the general reader should have, that he may realize in some degree the position of a prisoner at Andersonville, and to show that anything originally devised for our welfare might be perverted to our misery.

CHAPTER IX.

IT was in July that I first noticed negro prisoners among us, though they were, doubtless, there previous to that time. Scarcely any of them but were victims of atrocious amputations performed by rebel surgeons. It was said that none of the prisoners were captured except the wounded. Those in the prison were mostly New England men. Some of them had been captured at the charge on Fort Wagner, when Colonel Shaw was killed, and at the battle of Olustee, Florida. I observed in the negro prisoners a commendable trait of cleanliness. Indeed, I may safely say, their clothes were, on an average, cleaner and better patched than those of other prisoners of the stockade. Through exposure to the sun and rain, they were much blacker than the common southern negroes, and many were the exclamations of surprise among the guard at this fact. "The blackest niggers I ever saw," was the common expression on seeing them. I have said the negroes were mostly wounded and mutilated; when there had been a case of amputation, it had been performed in such a manner as to twist and distort the limb out of shape. When a negro was placed in a squad among white men, it was usually accompanied with the injunction, addressed to the sergeant of the squad, "Make the d—d nigger work for and wait upon you : if he does not, lick him, or report him to me, and I will." I never knew an instance, however, where a sergeant required of the black any service not usually allotted to others, and that in drawing and distributing rations.

Understanding that there was a major of colored troops in prison, I hunted him up, and found Major Archibald Bogle, who was formerly, I believe, a Lieutenant in the 17th Mass. infantry. He was captured at Olustee, after being severely wounded in several places. He informed me that he formerly lived in Melrose, Mass. Since he came into the pen, he had been refused all medical and surgical treatment, though the prisoners detailed as hospital stewards had covertly afforded him aid, and dressed his wounds. He wore his uniform, and freely declared himself an officer of negro troops — a fact which all officers of negroes were not willing to own, by reason of the hard treatment received therefor from the rebels. His was an instance of the fact that a true gentleman remains the same amidst the most squalid misery and accumulated misfortunes. His intercourse with others was dignified, courteous, and urbane, as if in command of his regiment. There were many in prison, as there always has been in our army, who professed to despise negro troops, and have a contempt for their officers. Major Bogle was, at one time, I was informed, compelled to mess with his negroes; yet he always maintained his gentlemanly bearing and his self-respect, and commanded the respect of others amid all the accumulated misery of the "prison pen." Such were my impressions of Major Bogle.

Many loose statements have been made in print indicating that officers were as common among prisoners at Andersonville as enlisted men. With the exception of Major Bogle, there were no commissioned officers intentionally placed in Andersonville. Others were there by their own act; but the prison was intended for enlisted men only. At any time an officer of white troops could be sent to Macon, or some other officers' prison, by merely making a plain statement of facts which looked plausible. So much is required to be said, as there seems to be a great misunderstanding in relation to this matter; and it is my desire to write such a description of the prison that those who were prisoners at the time with myself will be the ones most

11

ready to testify to the truth of these pictures, crudely
drawn with pen and ink. Major Bogle, at one time,
was engaged in a tunnelling operation, in which he
plotted to release all the prisoners of the stockade. It
failed through the treason of some one in the secret,
though it came near being a success. About the time
I became acquainted with him, an extensive plot was
formed to break the stockade. Over two thousand men
were pledged to risk their lives upon an effort to liberate the prisoners of the stockade. Here seemed the
choice before us, to die without an effort, amid all the
misery of the prison pen, or to die with our hands up-
lifted to strike one blow at our enemies, before death,
in an attempt to liberate ourselves and starving comrades. To no reasonable man did there appear at that
time to be any hope for life but in that manner. I
went into the project, I am willing to confess at this
day, having full confidence in our ability to achieve the
desired result, and with a feeling that it was better to
die in such an attempt than to die a miserable, loathsome death by gradual starvation.

Acting in concert, we set ourselves at work, and dug
tunnels up to the stockade; then the tunnel branched
off at right angles, running parallel with the stockade,
a shoulder of earth being left as a temporary support,
so that when a rush was made against the walls from
the outside, it would be thrown down in the places thus
mined. In this manner three portions of the stockade
walls were undermined — at least, I have reason to

suppose so, although I was engaged in digging and engineering on but one of them. Our plans were as follows : One detachment of prisoners was to break through on the south side, near the gate, and capture the reserve of the guard; another to break through on the north side, and, making a circuit of the stockade, capture the guard thereon; another party, breaking through on the south-west side, near the gate, was to capture the rebel artillery near headquarters, and use it according to circumstances, and make such capture of rebel officers as was possible; while prisoners outside, under detail, were to cut the telegraph wires. This achieved, prisoners were to be liberated, rations equally distributed, the cars seized, ammunition and arms placed in the hands of "the organization," and then, raiding through the rebel country, seize upon horses and other modes of transportation, and effect an escape to the Gulf. Such were our plans generally.

All was pronounced ready for the grand assault, and we were waiting with trembling expectancy, when a proclamation was read in prison, and posted in conspicuous places, stating that such a plan was known to be organized, and the commandant of the prison had full knowledge of all its details, even to the names of those concerned; and that, if we persisted in carrying it out, there would be great bloodshed, which he wished to avert. Such, in substance, was a proclamation signed by Henry Wirz. We had been betrayed by one who, we supposed, from every motive of interest, would keep

the secret.   Artillery was posted at various points, with
men in position to use it : twice shots were fired over
the heads of prisoners in crowds, while white flags were
placed all over the prison, as ranges for their artillerists.
Thus ended the best-conceived plan for liberating the
prisoners *en masse* during my imprisonment, and proved
the assertion frequently made among the Kentucky
boys, that "Everything in the Confederacy was drefful
onsartain, and liable to bust."

After the repeated failure of long-cherished and hard-
worked plans, which were to give liberty or death to
the projectors, for once I became despondent and doubt-
ing, falling away from faith in ever getting out of prison
otherwise than by dying.   Dark clouds of despair
gathered around me, and followed my feeble footsteps.
Though I knew I was bringing upon myself the very
fate I had been so long trying to avert; knew that
such moods were productive of none but evil to him
who entertained them ; yet, for a time, it seemed impossible for me to rally from or shake them off.   In this
wretched condition of mind — prolific of none but per-
nicious results — I was, one day, creeping down the
slippery pathway of the hill, which led to the brook-
side.   Everything around me looked foreboding; the
dying men, who always encircled the quagmire of the
prison, stretched out their withered hands in supplication for food, which I had no power to give ; the dead,
lying with unclosed eyes and dirt-stained, pallid faces,
brought back to my heart, with startling force, the

question, How soon shall I, like these, lie uncared for, dead, starved, after a painful life without a gleam of hope? The thought was maddening; reason was tottering; and, full of half-formed, desperate thoughts and gloomy resolves of ending at once that which seemed must be ended there in long and torturing misery by starvation, I saw lying at my feet a bit of waste paper. I said within myself, If there is anything on that paper—one word of hope—I'll take courage and live; otherwise—and here I clutched the paper, when the first words that caught my eye were these:—

"Ye fearful saints, fresh courage take;
  The clouds ye so much dread
Are big with *mercy*, and will break
  With blessings on your head!"

It was a portion of the leaf of an old hymn book. I never saw the hymn before nor since, and I may not have quoted it exactly; yet, had an angel from heaven assured me of my ultimate release from rebel hands, I could not, thereafter, have been more confident of my destiny. Never, after that, did my faith waver even for an instant. At another time, one of my companions, seeking for encouragement in his despondency, placed, at random, his finger between the leaves of his Bible; it rested upon the twelfth verse of the one hundred and fortieth Psalm: "I know that the Lord will maintain the cause of the afflicted and the right of the poor." Of course hope always construed such omens on our side to our advantage. Thus it was that the prisoner clung to every straw of hope. At various times, when I first went into prison, I had jocosely taken little bets of suppers, dinners, &c., as to the duration of our imprisonment, but always lost them, through the death of the other party.

During the last of July, or first of August, an addition was made to the stockade. This gave to the thirty-five thousand crowded into the space of ten acres more room by ten additional acres. The opening of the new stockade, as it was usually termed, was an event which contributed to the comfort of the prisoners in various ways. It gave them more wood, by the tearing down of the stockade walls, which had separated the new enclosure from the old, furnishing for a time a good supply. But, as the majority in prison had no means of splitting and cutting up the huge logs which formed the stockade walls, nor the instruments for digging up or cutting down the huge timbers, the bottoms of which had been solidly fixed into the ground some eight feet, and as but a limited number of the thirty thousand men could work at such employment at a time, the supply fell into the hands of a few who had the strength and implements to do the work. The stock, however, was soon exhausted, and wood became almost as scarce as ever. There were yet in the new stockade roots and stumps, which gave, for a while, to those who had the courage and strength to dig in the hot sun, a supply. But the larger number had neither strength, courage, nor the implements, other than their fingers, to dig with.

The reader, in considering our circumstances, must always remember that the great majority of the imprisoned thousands had become so emaciated and weak by continual exposure and starvation as to be scarcely able to take advantage of any circumstance like the foregoing in their favor. There were always a few, perhaps one in two hundred, who formed an exception to the great mass of sufferers. A few who had axes or large wedges were able, in some cases, to lay in a large supply of wood, but, as want increased, these did not long retain possession. The police, vigilant in all matters of general interest to themselves, caused those thus stocked to divide with the suffering thousands around them, taking a good share for their own trouble. With all the additional acres added to the prison grounds, we were still crowded for room; and if I have not continually impressed the reader with our miserably cramped condition, it was because one statement of such facts seemed sufficient. For two or three weeks there was a better supply of wood, but soon it was as scarce as ever.

In spite of the sufferings endured, which I have but feebly portrayed in the preceding pages, any offered relief that involved dishonor to themselves, or reflected discredit on our government, was not favorably received by the great mass of suffering men. At one time, during a period of most intense suffering, rebels from Macon and other large places came into the stockade, offering tempting inducements for prisoners to go with them, and work, during their imprisonment, at their trades. Shoemakers, carpenters, blacksmiths, and coopers were offered good food, clothes, and liberal compensation in greenbacks. Those who made this proposition were actually mobbed, and forced to leave the prison, by men who were on the brink of starvation, who had partaken of but one scanty meal during forty-eight hours. I observed, from time to time, in the different prisons where propositions were made of this nature, that a time was always selected when we were suffering the most for want of food. It was possible — and the fact speaks volumes in favor of the prisoners' fidelity to the government — they knew that at any other time such propositions would be rejected with contempt. The common sentiment among prisoners was, that it was as bad to assume the places of men who would thus be enabled to take muskets, as to use up arms themselves against their country.

David Robinson was a middle-aged man, a mechanic of Massachusetts, who had left a family at home dependent upon him for support, to fight the battles of the country. His son, a lad of eighteen years, a fine, manly fellow as ever gladdened a father's heart, had followed in his footsteps. When the proposition came to go out to work, and thus save the life of himself and son, he replied, "No! I know for what I enlisted, and have been fighting for; the boy and I will die, but we can never desert the cause." The boy died, in what manner I shall relate in coming pages. The father, broken in heart and health, lives to mourn his son. Yet he was only a New England mechanic, whom the terrors of death could not seduce from his country's cause. At another time the proposition was made to Corporal Gibson, of my company, an old man, who afterwards died at Charleston. The answer was heroic: "You can starve my body, but shall not stain my soul with treason!" Such were the men who died by thousands, and filled the begrudged graves dug by relentless foes.

During July and August efforts were persistently made by men among us, backed by the rebels, to get up a petition representing our condition, and asking our government to take action for our release. This was, in my opinion, at the time, and also that of a great majority in the prison, but an effort of the rebels to make the misery inflicted by themselves subservient to their own base purposes of forcing our government to their own terms. In prison, as elsewhere, there was a diversity of opinion, yet the almost unanimous voice was against forwarding such a petition. Sergeant Kellogg, I believe it was, who was captured at Plymouth, was asked to sign it. "No," he replied; "our government will do what is right. These are our enemies, trying to benefit their cause, not yours." Such was the language of starving patriots, and such was the force of words fitly spoken, that they were repeated through the prison in reply to those who asked for signatures. Thus, often sterling words counteracted evil influences!

The rebels have since made a virtue of having forwarded, through kindred tools, such a petition. They could look on and see the prisoner starve, and rejoice thereat, without lifting a helping hand, and the next moment forward a petition to our government, setting forth the misery which they were inflicting! Towards those of our own numbers who were forced by hunger to be their tools, we should be charitable, yet I believe it to be a fact, that those who signed that petition, were those who were suffering least in prison, — bounty-jumpers and deluded men, — men not in sympathy with the cause. The great mass repudiated the petition, and to-day, when the old flag floats over every foot of land once desecrated by rebels, I feel a thrill of pleasure, — melancholy though it be, — in contemplating those dark days when men starved and dying would not swerve from the right, that the cause for which they died has triumphed. And in coming days, the noblest monuments of sacrifices made for the nation's safety shall be those patriots' graves!

The more the prisoners were abused, the more fondly did their thoughts turn to the old flag, under which they had fought, and which was the symbol of happiness and plenty at home. "We have confidence in our government," was a remark often made in reply to accusations by the rebels that our government did not care whether we starved or not. When I consider that this was the common language of men suffering under miseries rarely, if ever, paralleled in history; I cannot be astonished that the Union exists to-day. I feel a conscious joy that there was no act of mine, during a bitter imprisonment, to disgrace that flag. In referring to the North, as distinguished from the South, it was often spoken of as "God's country," and the old flag as "God's flag." Such was the halo of glory with which all its associations seemed surrounded.

Incidents were of such frequent occurrence pathetically illustrative of the prisoners' devotion to the glorious Stars and Stripes, that I will narrate one expressive of the form this devotion often took. A color-sergeant of one of the regiments captured at Plymouth, N. C., died some time in August. While his companions were rendering the last services, — that rude preparation for the grave already described, — they discovered his regimental flag, which he had so often borne in battle, wrapped about his person. He had placed it secretly there to shield it from traitor hands. He could not bear that this loved symbol of his country's glory should be desecrated by the hands of traitors. Reverently his comrades gazed upon its folds, and silently, with tearful eyes, again restored it, as a fit covering for his noble breast, to be buried with him. A glorious winding sheet for a patriot! Dying men clung to little mementoes, such as a miniature flag, or the badge of their army corps. But it was the general constancy with which men ever clung through all their misery, with love to their country and its cause, which spoke more eloquently than any mere incident of their devotion, and the triumph of principles over circumstances of misery.

CHAPTER X.

Exchange on the Brain. — Rumors of Sherman's Movements. — Great Expectations and sad Results. — Fearful Mortality. — Hot Sun and powerful Rains. — Stockade swept away. — A Spring of pure Water. — A new Tunnelling Operation nearly fatal to its Projectors. — Rebel Aid for once welcomed. — Construction of rude Barracks. — Prospects of Winter in Prison not encouraging. — Weary, miserable Days. — Increased Sickness and Mortality. — Names of fifty deceased in the Writer's Company. — Contrast of Loyal Blacks with Disloyal Whites. — Another Tunnelling Operation betrayed for Tobacco. — The Betrayer punished. — Believed to be a Spy. — Further Rumors of Exchange. — A Realization. — Great Joy. — Dying Comrade when Release was ordered. — An affecting Scene. — Delusive Hopes. — Departure from Andersonville. — Short Rations. — Doubtful Deliverance. — Charleston again. — A Talk with a Rebel Citizen. — Effects of the Siege on the City. — Pity and Sympathy. — Shot and Shell a Civilizer. — The Fair Grounds.

HERE, as in other prisons, a fearful epidemic reigned, termed by old prisoners "Exchange on the Brain." Frequent rumors of exchange were circulated designedly by the rebels, for the purpose of quieting desperate men, and preventing the formation of dangerous plots for release and escape. Often these rumors seemed to have some foundation. Once the priest who had charge of the spiritual development of the prison commander, Wirz, came into prison, and read to a large concourse of prisoners, gathered to hear, extracts from a paper purporting to give news of an exchange about to take place at Savannah. · Prisoners coming in from Sherman's army brought news of a raid under Stoneman and McCook. The next news we heard was, that Stoneman's cavalry was fighting around Macon; and then it was announced by exultant Johnnies, that Stoneman and his whole army were captured. This was partially confirmed by men belonging to his force, coming in as captives. They informed us of the siege of Atlanta, and reiterated the former news of an exchange agreed upon; but when and where it was to take place, they had no information. When Stoneman was raiding towards us, with evident intentions of releasing the prisoners; when rumors came of his having arms for the prisoners, — which I have since ascertained to be true, — our hearts beat high with hope. Those who had previously had tendencies of Exchange on the Brain, went fearfully wild with release in the same place. A few, who had learned by bitter experience how uncertain every thing in Dixie was, while cheered by bright prospects, put but little real confidence in them. Some pinned their faith and hopes so implicitly upon a release, that they were unwilling to wait even a day, and when at last they found their hopes and faith disappointed, sunk into a despondency from which nothing could arouse them, and died. Rumors and statements of an exchange were so frequently made and backed by evidence which looked plausible, that the prisoners were expectant and despondent by turns during July and August.

These two months were the most terrible of any experienced by the general prisoners. Nine thousand were said to have died during that space of time. In one day in August, no less than one hundred and sixty prisoners died, and the average was over a hundred daily. From the 1st of February to the 16th of September, twelve thousand Federal soldiers, prisoners of war, were carried from the prison to the dead man's trench and the felon's burial. Many of the deaths were hastened by despondency. After an usual excitement about exchange, — expecting to be called out to be released at any moment, — followed by disappointment, deaths were the most frequent.

Extreme heat, during July and August, was often followed by days dark with intermittent showers. On one occasion, during such a period, the ground was rendered so hot by the intense rays of the sun as to blister my feet by mere contact. This period of heat was followed by rain in such quantities as in a few hours to cause a freshet, which swept away the stockade where the brook entered and left the prison; and also swept away portions on the north-west side, by the flowing of the water down the hill-side. Wretched creatures all over the prison were crawling out of holes in the ground, in which they had burrowed, half drowned with the water which had suddenly filled them. Canteens, plates, bits of wood, blankets, spoons, pails, and hats,

were swept away down the hill-side, the prisoners
franticly rushing after their deserting goods and habitations. The only washing some of the poor fellows got
was on such an occasion. It was curious to observe
the different manner in which various individuals
accepted of such a dispensation. Some laughed, others
swore and abused fate, many screamed and cried as if
mad, while still others crouched in the rain, or saw the
whole scene unmoved, as if gazing on a panorama with
which they had no concern. I sat at such times crouching in the rain, my body bent up in a manner to bring
my knees, stomach, and head in close contact, between
which were folded and placed my jacket and ragged
blanket, — my back exposed to the rain, forming a kind
of roof to keep these valuables from the wet. But all
in vain such an effort. The force of the rain, running
down the hill-side, continually upset me, by under-
mining the sand beneath my feet, until at last losing
my blanket and philosophy, miserable and grotesque as
others, I went rushing and pitching after my tin pail
and blanket, caught up and carried away by the
torrent.

Large forces were thrown out to protect the portions
of stockade swept away by the flood, and keep the
prisoners from desperate attempts at escape. All night
under arms these forces were kept in position in the
rain, until the stockade was repaired. Night and day
artillery was manned, which commanded the broken
portions of the stockade, and every precaution taken

against the escape of prisoners. One great good resulted from this freshet.   On the hill-side where the
stockade had been broken away, a spring was discovered, which supplied an abundance of pure water to the
prisoners, greatly in contrast with the filthy stream
which had been our only supply during the summer.

Shortly after the foregoing event, I became engaged
in a tunnelling operation, which came near proving
fatal to its projector.   Tunnels did not usually cave in,
for these reasons : the top of the earth, after the tunnel
passed under the dead line, was interlaced by roots and
fibres, which formed sufficient adhesive power, in most
parts of the stockade, to keep the earth from caving in.
Besides, the earth was usually hard and clayey.   In
this case, however, after we got beyond the stockade,
on the outside, we ran into sandy soil, where our misfortunes began.   Two of us were digging, in the day-
time, when, in our rear, the tunnel caved in, and
effectually cut off our retreat into the stockade.   Gradually it commenced falling upon us, filling our ears,
eyes, and mouths with dirt.   There seemed to be no
release from our critical condition, except by digging
upward, which we commenced to do with fear and
trembling, as that operation was always attended with
great danger of being buried alive.   Suddenly, down
came a mass of earth above us, which did not, as we
anticipated, bury us so deep but that we scrambled
out of it, shrieking with terror.   The rebel guard at
that time, coming around with the relief, rescued us

12

from our peril — the only time I was ever glad to see a rebel.

During the last of August, rude barracks were in process of construction in the upper portion of the new stockade. This looked like preparations for winter, and gave us but little comfort, as these buildings consisted of roofs only, on uprights, and there was no prospect of more than a very few being accommodated by their use.

The weary, weary, dreadful days dragged slowly along, amid suffering and death in prison. September came. Over fifty of my company had died since the term of imprisonment began, which was not so large in proportion to their number as occurred in other companies captured at the same time with ourselves. The majority of our two companies were veterans — strong men, inured to hardships and exposure by a previous experience in camp and field. Scarcely any of my company died until after the middle of July; August swept them away by scores. The following is an incomplete, imperfect list of those who died: Wm. Arrington, Wm. Bessom, Nicholas Bessom, Chas. A. Bent, Wm. Brown, Winslow A. Bryant, B. G. M. Dyer, Wm. H. Burns, Geo. Combs, Peter Dunn, John Duffee, B. W. Drake, Geo. Edwards, Geo. Floyd, John Fegan, Cyrus B. Fisher, Patrick Flynn, James Henry, G. P. Reed, S. A. Smith, John Shaw, J. Thomas, James Wilson, C. O. Wilson, F. A. Stephens, G. Arrington, Pat. Henley, Charles Holbrook, Joseph Hoyt, Wm. H.

Haynes, Wm. Johnson, Michael Kelleher, Chas. A. Moore, Wm. McGrain, Chas. Moss, John Milan, Bernard Mehan, C. M. Martin, John McDermot, John Nevison, Benj. Phillips, Chandler Petie, Patrick Regan, Wm. Wyman, Kendal Piersons, Wm. L. Gordon, and others whose names I have lost.

Poor boys! Noble fellows! As I recall their names, memory brings each face, pale with prison suffering, before me. I cannot but have greater faith in human nature from having known them. Dear comrades! endeared to me by many sufferings! guilty of no crimes; theirs was a death of lingering torture, to which, in comparison, the devices of the Inquisition would have been mercy. Victims of a relentless hatred which has not ceased with the war, your nameless, crowded graves dot the prison burial-ground, and point a solemn moral to the barbarities enacted there. To-day, when the men of Georgia ask the rights they formerly exercised, and among them the right of excluding the negro from the ballot-box, I wonder those patriot bones do not start from their crowded, shallow graves, to bear testimony that, while living, every white man of that locality banded with bloodhounds to prevent their escape, forming a network of vigilance through which it was almost an impossibility to break, and their only dependence was in the blacks, — the Unionists alone of that section, — who harbored them when it was a peril to their lives, and gave them of their food when they had but a bare subsistence for themselves. You who sit by the quiet fireside and read these records of suffering, reflect, when you hear the clamorings of those who are trying to regain lost power, that they are those who, all over that southern land, by their silence con-. sented, or by action indorsed, the barbarous treatment under which Union men lingered, suffered and died amid the tortures of starvation.

In September my last effort at gaining liberty by tunnelling was frustrated. Fifty men commenced a tunnel on a grand scale. It was nearly completed, and was the most perfect thing of the kind ever devised by the prisoners. It was commenced at the bottom of an old well, and two men could walk abreast from one end to the other. One of our number betrayed us to the rebel quartermaster for a plug of tobacco. Another of our companions saw them conversing, and, getting behind them, heard him propose to tell the quartermaster something important, if he would give him the tobacco. He ran and informed us in season for us to make ourselves scarce. After the tunnel was discovered, those engaged in it were naturally enraged, and, seizing the traitor, printed on his forehead, with India ink and needles, indelibly, the letter T. They were proceeding to worse punishment, when a rebel guard came into the stockade and carried him outside. In spite of evidence to the contrary, I have but little doubt he was a rebel spy, who had been sent in with other prisoners to betray us. Diligent inquiries were set on foot to find out who had punished the traitor in the manner described. To accomplish this, we were threatened with being starved into submission; but the rations, after being stopped for twenty-four hours, were again issued.

Rumors of exchange continued to pervade the prison. Men, crazy with the idea of freedom and home, wandered up and down the prison, clinging to every rumor, like drowning men to straws. The excitement was made worse by the extravagant rumor circulated around camp by the rebel quartermaster and the priest, who was said to be Wirz's confessor! The excitement increased daily, and men were expecting at any moment to be called out. Many were called, but it was to that bourn from whence no traveller returns: many were released, but the herald of their freedom was the grim messenger, Death!

At last, after repeated rumors had prepared the prison for their purpose, orders came for certain of the detachments, or nineties, as they were termed, to be ready to leave the prison. We were told that there was a Federal transport fleet off Savannah, waiting for us. To all in prison this seemed the dawn of freedom, and the most incredulous believed. Kentucky Joe, who always protested that everything was "dreadful onsartain in Dixie," became a convert, and had exchange on the brain. Every one clamored for a chance, and feared to be left out of the exchange. Ninety after ninety went out of prison rejoicing, and faintly cheering. It was cheering which brought tears to the eye, so puny and weak did it come from the poor, weak, starved fellows.　But

> " The hollow eye grew bright,
> And the poor heart almost gay,
> As they thought of seeing home and friends again."

I never hear that song without its recalling that scene. Men who had been brought by suffering to the very verge of idiocy, or who for months had been smitten with almost hopeless melancholy or despair, as these sounds came at last dimly to their ear, like remembrance of a dream, their glorious import, "going home," burst upon them.　They staggered to their feet, and were carried, by the pressure of a dense crowd, outside the prison, feebly cheering, or regardless of the presence of rebels, joined in the chorus of

> " Rally round the flag, boys, rally once again."

My ninety had got orders to be ready, and I was in a tremor of excitement, when one of my comrades sent for me, saying he was dying.　My heart sank at thinking of the suffering, dying men who must stay behind and perish.　My heart almost reproached me for being glad, when companions who had stood by my side in days of battle were suffering — dying, with none to care for them, — without sister's or mother's hand to soothe them, without food, and with no shelter from the pitiless rain and sun.

I went, and found John Nevison stretched on the

poor remains of his blanket, dying. How often the poor fellow, true to a stubborn Scotch nature, had rallied, and tried to live! "I am glad you are going home, Sarge." (His generous heart had room for joy at others' good fortune even in death.) "I wish you to send word to my mother" (Mrs. Margaret Nevison, Newcastle, England, on the Tyne); "tell her I enlisted to fight against slavery—for my adopted country. Tell her all about me!" Poor fellow! I understood him; he wished me to tell her he had done his duty. Comrade in battle, I can testify that none stood up in fight more manfully than John Nevison — he who so often had sung, with pathetic voice, the song,

> "Comrades, will you tell me, truly,
> Who shall care for *mother* now?"

I now understood why he sung that song with so much feeling. He never before had spoken of his mother. Poor John! enshrined in the hearts of comrades, you lie in your nameless grave among the victims of Andersonville; and

> "Who will care for mother now?"

I took his poor, thin hand in mine, and pledged him I would do all he wished. I forgot his address for a time, but in the delirium of a fever recalled it, though many other forgotten things were not again brought to mind.

I was waiting for my turn to come to get out of

prison. Every subterfuge was resorted to to go with the lucky ones. Those who had means bribed; those who had none "flanked," and were rewarded ofttimes with broken heads, for others became savage at the idea of being cheated out of their chance, and the police exercised anything but a protecting influence upon the unlucky heads of flankers. Those who tried their wits received often a reminder upon their brain, not as a test of its quality, but as a check to its further exercise. Men were crying at the gate, as we went out, at being defrauded of their chance by some audacious flanker. I went at last, rejoicing at what appeared to be the day of deliverance. As I passed rebel headquarters, I saw Sergeant Smith, who, it will be remembered, was one of my captors when I escaped at one time from Andersonville. "Well, Smith," said I, "there are no bloodhounds after me this trip homeward." The Sergeant shook his head (it seems to me, sorrowfully, when I recall it now) to see us thus elated by delusive hopes of "going home," destined, O, in how many cases, never to be realized! We reached the depot, were divided into squads of sixty, and crowded into box cars. We were full of hope, however, and kept saying, "Well, we shall have room enough soon." Our rations had been previously placed in each car — a piece of corn-cake about the shape and size of a brick. We were told these were our rations for three days' journey. One of my comrades, J. W. D., desperately resolved to preserve a piece of the bread to carry home as a curiosity; but hunger got the better of the poor fellow's resolve, and I saw the last crumb disappearing before the afternoon of our second day's journey.

During the first day, three men died in the car where I was. My bread lasted me two days, as I was careful not to eat too much at a time; yet it was considerable trouble to have it around — a continual temptation to myself and to others. We arrived at Macon the afternoon of our first day's travel. The vigilance of the guard was here redoubled, and the fact excited our suspicion that there was to be no exchange, after all. As we passed through Macon, one of Stoneman's men pointed out to me the bullet marks on the buildings and fences made by our advance just before his capture. We had been suspicious that we were going to Alabama, but our hearts rose within us as the cars took the direction for Savannah. A negro informed us that "Captin Sherman" had taken Atlanta, and was making for Macon as "tight as he can come." This looked like removing us to a place of security rather than an exchange; still, we were hopeful that we were to be exchanged to prevent our capture. As we neared Savannah, and changed our guard, the officer of the new guard came up, and we made inquiries of him as to our destination — if we were to be exchanged. He replied by candidly stating that we were to be placed down on one of the islands, under fire from the Federal guns. Several men were shot, on our route from Savannah to Charleston, while trying to escape from the cars. We caught sight of our fleet in the distance, as we passed over the bridge leading to Charleston, — and our hearts thrilled with a savage kind of joy, when we heard the shell from our batteries, shrieking over the city. We termed them Gilmore's errand boys, or Gilmore's morning reports on the condition of rebeldom.

At last the cars were halted in the streets of Charleston, and citizens, negroes, and soldiers, thronging the streets, peered curiously into the cars, to get a look at the Yanks. It appeared to me, then, that they wore a haggard, care-worn look. The only hopeful face of the group was some old negress, who had kept fat and jolly on the idea of Uncle Abe's coming soon. Said one citizen to another, in my hearing, "They are all foreigners — ain't they?" This riled me not a little, and I replied, saying, "You recollect the Plymouth prisoners who passed through these streets in April?" "Yes, perfectly; a very fine body of men," said he. "These are the same men; your government has starved all semblance of men out of us." "You are a foreigner?" said he, looking sneeringly and critically at my dilapidated wardrobe and dirty face, which had been guiltless of washing for the three days of our journey. "No, I belong to Massachusetts!" I proudly replied. He seemed much shocked, either at the fact of our condition, or that any one should not be ashamed to hail from Massachusetts.

It was just before sundown when we were formed in line, and marched through the back streets of Charleston. The effects of the siege were visible upon every hand, but we were informed that the damage done was really worse than mere appearances indicated. The shell made only an irregular hole through the exterior walls, whereas the interior of buildings where shell had exploded was often a mass of ruins. It was no figure of speech, but a reality, that grass was growing in the streets of the proud but doomed city which first raised its defiant hand against the Federal government. The shell and shot from Gilmore's batteries had a civilizing influence over its people, for in no place were we so kindly treated by citizens and soldiers as in Charleston. Women and children looked pityingly upon us, and such expressions as "Poor fellows!" "Too bad!" &c., showed pity and sympathy for our condition, which we had never before experienced in the Confederacy.

I noticed that those citizens whose dress betokened that they belonged to the better classes wore often a sober, subdued look, which, during my experience in the war, I had observed as the result of much anxiety, mental suffering, and loss of friends. I addressed one of these as we were waiting on the street — "Ain't you folks about sick of all this fighting?" "We are tired of it, dreadful sick of it," said he, while he vainly tried to keep back the tears that ran down his face; "but we are going to fight you'un Yanks just as long as we kin." Noble stuff — worthy of a more decent cause.

Finally, just as the sun was setting in an ocean of

beautiful clouds, we arrived at our destination on the " Fair Ground," or "Race Course," in the rear of Charleston, where were about five thousand of the Andersonville prisoners, who had preceded us. The situation was pleasant; the green grass, to which our sight had been unused for many weary months, met the eye with refreshing pleasantness. The situation was better than we had anticipated, though we were disappointed in not being placed down on the islands, where we could see the flash of friendly artillery, or perchance the old flag, for no one who has not had such experience can understand the longing of our hearts for the old flag, and for familiar sights.

CHAPTER XI.

THE Fair Ground proper, when seen under favorable circumstances, must have been a beautiful spot. It contained an area of about forty acres, surrounded by dense overhanging trees, interwoven by ivy, laurel, and honeysuckle, forming an almost impenetrable foliage. Aside from a distant view, we were not allowed any of the enjoyments which such shade and beauty could confer. We were placed in the centre of the Fair Ground, with no shade or habitations, except such as we might construct from our garments or ragged blankets; but there was a cool breeze from the ocean, and the sound of bells and the rattle over pavements came pleasantly to the ear. The sight of green foliage refreshed the gaze of miserable men, for a long time unused to pleasant sights and sounds.

The night of our arrival, three "hard-tack" were issued as rations, for twenty-four hours, to each man, and we were in the third heavens in anticipating such luxurious rations each succeeding day. That night, after devouring two of my "hard crackers," I lay down to rest with the remaining one in my tin pail, under my head, for my morning's breakfast. I found it impossible to keep my mind from the hard-tack long enough to get to sleep, supposing some one would steal it while I was slumbering: the thought was maddening. Vainly I endeavored to divert my mind from craving hunger, by saying the multiplication-table. It was "no go." That hard-tack was so fascinating! Hunger, and fear of losing it, got the better of the contest with sleep, and I could bear no more. Arousing myself, I devoured that "infantry square," in one time and several motions, not down in the tactics. I never remember of enjoying any food, however luxurious, as I did that hard cracker.

I mention this incident, insignificant in itself, as illustrative of how little it took to elate or depress men in our condition. That night, however, I met with the great misfortune of my imprisonment. Some vagabond stole my little tin pail, which, I may say without exaggeration, had been my best friend during the preceding months of my captivity. It had been such a convenience to myself and companions, that few, who have not been prisoners, can understand how great a loss it was. Used by one and another, sometimes it was not off a fire during the day, except long enough to change hands.

I was reduced, by this misfortune, thenceforward through my imprisonment, to the unpleasant alternative of borrowing cooking utensils, or of eating my rice, flour, or Indian meal raw. It took so little in prison to make one's circumstances indescribably miserable, that this really was an overwhelming misfortune. The loss of a fortune at home could not have so affected my well-being or "good standing" among companions. From one accustomed to confer favors on others, I became dependent, and begging and hunting, often for whole days, for some one willing to loan me a tin quart to cook in.

On the morning following, the people of Charleston came in flocks to see the Yankees. A majority of these were women. Some few came with food to sell, but were not allowed to trade over the guard line with prisoners. Others, actuated by pity, watched for chances, and, when the rigor of the guard was relaxed, threw cakes, potatoes, or some like luxuries, over the guard line among the wretched creatures who gathered waiting for luck to favor them in some manner. The food thus thrown in was, however, but a drop in that Maelstrom of human miserables, who, actuated by hunger, struggled madly among each other for its possession. After a time, this feeding of the common prisoners was stopped, and the women were told to confine their manifestations of pity to the hospital, which was situated outside of the prison grounds, in our rear. Many a poor fellow, who otherwise would have died, lives to bless the women of Charleston. May those whose hands were thus lifted in pity never be stricken down with that hopeless hunger which they sought so kindly to relieve!

The next evening we received as rations two "hardtack" per man, and a rarity of about two ounces of fresh meat, — which last was, so far as I observed, eaten raw throughout the camp at one sitting. Thus it was that we were inclined to be pleased with the change in our situation, in spite of disappointment about exchange. During the first two weeks, I had not been fortunate enough to get the means of constructing shelter. One day, when wood was being brought to the camp for the use of the prison, I accosted an officer, whom I saw around camp, and requested him to get me three sticks from the wood-pile, that I might construct a shelter from the sun by raising my blanket upon them. Contrary to my expectations, he at once kindly complied with my wishes, and I was made happy with the means of constructing a "shebang." Upon subsequent inquiry, I found this officer to be Lieutenant-Colonel Iverson, in command of the camp. He had very strong prejudices against Yankees, but was inclined to do all within his limited power to better the condition of the prisoners.

At Charleston we obtained a kind of brackish water, by digging shallow wells from six to ten feet deep. In a short time, so easy were they to dig, they became so plenty as to be annoying and inconvenient to the pedestrians around camp. Plenty of water, coupled with the fact that, about twice a week, we got a small piece of soap, caused clean faces to become more common than ever before in prison. The inconvenience above mentioned was so great that one could not walk around in the evening without being precipitated into a well. Thus many a fellow took an extemporized bath, in which his feet and legs, or head and shoulders, got the uncontemplated benefit of water. Under such disadvantages, night-walking became unpopular and unpleasant.

Each morning, about sunrise, shell from the guns of the Federal batteries down the harbor would begin to burst over a prominent steeple of the city. The report of the gun which sent the missile could not usually be heard. These were termed, among the prisoners, Gilmore's morning reports. Sometimes a shell would burst over the Fair Ground, which would be received with great enthusiasm among the prison boys, and with demonstrations of applause, such as, "Bully for the Swamp Angel," &c. Some days the bombarding would be very active, and we could hear in the city the dull thud, and the ripping and tearing, as the shell penetrated or burst in buildings. As may be supposed, it was diverting to us to see and hear these evidences of retributive justice going on among our foes. If one had fallen in our very midst, I have no doubt our boys would have cried, "Bully!" so welcome, always, were these evidences of the nearness of friends. The people of Charleston seemed to have got accustomed to them to such a degree that, during the heaviest bombardment of September, when none cared to stay in the lower portion of the city, the boys were unconcernedly flying their kites. I counted eighteen kites up while one of the heaviest bombardments was going on. Fires were of such frequent occurrence, resulting from shells, that the fire department became almost as important as that of the military.

On the first week of my confinement at Charleston, our old enemy, the dead line, was introduced. A negro, superintended by the "irrepressible" white man, was sent around camp, turning a furrow with a plough and its mule attachment. This was the line which to overstep was death to the prisoner. None but those prisoners in comparatively good health had been sent from Andersonville. For quite a time an effort seemed to be made to relieve our misery; but the great mass had been starved and exposed to sun and rain too long to be benefited by anything short of a most radical change. Hence men died about as fast, in proportion to their numbers, as at Andersonville. Scurvy, diarrhœa, and fever swept the prisoners off in vast numbers.

The place dignified by being called "the hospital," did not contain a single tent, the only shelter being, here and there, blankets raised on sticks, which were inadequate protection from rain or sun. Colonel Iverson, who, I believe, was, for a time, in command of the prison, made strenuous efforts for our benefit. A sutler was appointed for the camp, who was not allowed to ask of prisoners higher prices than asked in the city. This was a convenience to those who had money, but the great majority had none. The sutler's store of goods contained but few varieties — black pepper, unground, turnips, sweet potatoes, and baker's bread. Ten dollars in Confederate money for one in greenbacks was the general rate of exchange; and this was obtained through the Sisters of Charity, who visited us, doing acts of kindness to the suffering, bringing clothes and food, carrying messages to our officers, prisoners in the city, and bringing the reply. To people so cleanly we must have been objects of disgust. The vermin, visible upon all prisoners, could not have been pleasant to refined persons, unaccustomed to such misery. Our dirt-begrimed, half-naked persons must have been revolting, yet no word or look from these kindly Sisters showed shrinking or disgust. I have seen them bending in prayer or in offices of mercy over almost naked creatures, whom disease and filth had rendered indescribably loathsome, never, by word or look, showing other feeling than pity, and never making the object of their care feel humiliation or shame. Their kindly address of " My poor child ! " fell pleasantly on the ear. No importunities could vex them, and I do not remember of having heard an utterance of impatience from their lips. I may have been prejudiced, at first, against these Sisters of Charity, but certainly their acts were truly Christian, worthy of imitation by all on like occasions.

As I have said, gangrene, diarrhœa, and scurvy raged terribly in camp, notwithstanding our improved condition. It was about the third week of my stay at Charleston, I was told that Corporal Gibson, of my company, whom I have mentioned in preceding pages, lay dying. I found this brave man lying in the hot sun, with no shelter or attendant. Said he, " I could have lived to get out of the hands of any savages but these ; they are too cruel for an old man like me to expect from them anything less than death." The untold sufferings this man endured, — who once had refused to purchase freedom and life as the price of treason, — retaining clearness of mind until the moment of death, was but one instance among the many daily occurring in prison. A young soldier, who at one time had been clerk of Company G, second Massachusetts heavy artillery, died during the same week at Charleston. In his last moments he continually said, " I should be willing to die if I could have enough to eat, and die at home." Thus longings for home and food and thoughts of death were often bitterly crowded together.

For convenience in issuing rations, the prisoners were divided into detachments of thousands, and then subdivided into hundreds. There were sergeants of thousands and sergeants of hundreds, and a chief sergeant over the whole. These divisions were to facilitate the issue of rations, and the sergeants were selected from among the prisoners, and were often chosen by them. Much trouble, first and last, occurred in prison from the rebels never being able to count the prisoners correctly. We were often counted, but with no satisfactory results. There were, throughout the prison, so many hungry men — whose wits seemed to sharpen in proportion to their hunger — continually devising ways to get "extra feed," that it was not strange that the rebels frequently found themselves issuing more rations than there were men in prison. By judicious management, ingenious Yankees contrived to belong to two or more squads, and draw rations for each without exciting suspicion. Upon one count the rebel sergeants found they had issued five hundred more rations than there were men in camp ; and even by exercise of the greatest care in these countings, they would often be cheated two or three hundred men, through the dexterity which prisoners had acquired of shifting from one squad to another, and getting counted twice. Once, while endeavoring to count us, Colonel Iverson was so baffled by the tactics, that he dismissed the matter for the day, good naturedly declaring that we were "heavy dogs."

At last, in despair of finding out the exact number

of Yanks in any other manner, they marched the prisoners out into the open space, and kept us standing in line until counted; but even here, where any cheat seemed certain of being detected, and though threatened with punishment if we played Yankee tricks on them, the men of the rear rank were managed in such a manner that, in our detachment, a little over nine hundred men contrived to count up a thousand. The officer counting us mistrusted something wrong, and recounted us twice, without detecting the cheat, but expressed his distrust in a kind of a stage aside, saying, "You'n Yanks are the doggondest fellows I ever did count." The rebels in this transaction reminded me of Cuffee, who, being asked by his master if he had counted all the pigs, replied, "Yes, massa, all 'cept a little speckled one; he run'd round so I couldn't count him." They never succeeded to their liking in making us come out straight.

About this time Colonel Iverson detected the sutler in two offences: first, of receiving greenbacks in payment for goods, — a criminal offence in the Confederacy, — and, second, charging the prisoners exorbitant prices in trading. Whereupon he confiscated the greenbacks, to be used to obtain comforts for our sick, and forced him to conform to the schedule of prices in the city. The following were, with little variation, the prices charged in Confederate money: Bread, one dollar per loaf; sweet potatoes, ten dollars per bushel; three flat turnips, one dollar; black pepper, ten dollars per ounce. Taking into consideration the fact that one dollar in greenbacks would bring ten dollars in Confederate money, it made the schedule of prices extremely reasonable to those who were lucky enough to have money. There were, however, only a very few fortunate ones who had managed to conceal money, and get into prison with it. Those who had been captured during the summer in the vicinity of Richmond, underwent strict searches, and were robbed of their money, watches, and other valuables by the authorities, who pretended that they would again be restored when their imprisonment was over. Whatever may have been their intentions at the time, I never knew of but one instance where such promises were fulfilled, and that was in the case of Colonel Iverson, who had taken away greenbacks to the amount of many hundred dollars, and when the prisoners were released, restored the money. The great majority of prisoners had not a cent in their pockets, nor a pocket to put it in if they had a cent. To such the sale of the delicacies mentioned was nothing but an aggravation. If potatoes had sold for five cents a bushel, not more than one man in a hundred of the prisoners could have purchased a peck.

After giving us hard-tack for a few days, raw rations were issued in prison in very small quantities, in which the rebels seemed to have adopted a plan to make variety take the place of quantity. Rations for each man per day were for a time as follows: Two heaped spoonfuls of rice, two of flour, one of beans, and one of hominy. I remember it more particularly, as one of my comrades, who acted as a squad sergeant, usually divided the rations with a common teaspoon. Sometimes this estimate would fall short, but rarely, if ever, overrun. Wood was issued in quantities of about one common cord wood pine stick for twenty men per day. But its issue was very irregular. Sometimes none would be given for weeks. There was, however, a good excuse for this, for all the wood had to be brought a long distance on the cars, and then brought in teams to the prison ground. As there was a scarcity of rolling stock in those parts, this was a better excuse than could be found at Andersonville, where the prison was surrounded by a dense pine forest.

Many of the prisoners were destitute of cooking utensils, and could not borrow; and either from want of strength to run round, or getting discouraged by failures, after repeated rebuffs upon application for such favors, they would eat their rations raw, or go without. A young fellow belonging to the eighty-fifth New York independent battery, named Myers, had nothing in which to draw his rations, but a boot leg, into which he had fitted a wooden bottom. He had no cooking utensil, and ate his rations from this boot leg, without a spoon, day after day, uncooked, sometimes stirred up in a little water. This miserable being camped on the ground near the place I occupied. He scarcely ever lay down at night without wishing that he might never awake. It did, indeed, require more courage to live than to die. At last, after days and nights of lingering torture, his prayers for death were answered. Near me, one morning, I found his cold and lifeless form stretched upon the ground. He had died, his eyes closed as if in sleep. I noticed something clasped in his hand, and stooped to examine it. It was the likeness of a beautiful girl, and on the back was written in a delicate female hand, "To William, from Sarah" — a whole history of love, disappointment, and death, in brief. When I reflected that each man among the thousands dying around me had histories similar in their griefs, and loves, and longings for home, and when I considered the bitter pangs of dying men uncared for among worse than barbarians, it seemed too much of human misery for contemplation or utterance.

One day, when some Sisters of Charity came into the prison limits, — no very agreeable task for a cleanly female, — one of them remarked, in apology for not having got some article which she had undertaken to obtain for one of our number, that the firing was so heavy that it was not safe to venture down in the part of the city where such things were sold. These kindly Sisters attended to all alike without ever inquiring our creed, or appearing to think they were doing anything more than a duty.

My physical condition at this time was worse than at any time during my captivity. My clothes were in tatters, scurvy had drawn up the cords of my legs, and from the same cause my teeth were almost dropping from my jaws; my gums and mouth were swollen, and it became difficult to eat the most common food. My bones ached so intensely at times that I could find no more appropriate name for the pain than "teethache" in them. Something must be done. I must make continual efforts, or go down to the dogs' death many were suffering around me. So I used to wander around camp, picking up potato peelings from the mud and dirt, which some "well-to-do" fellow had thrown away. These I washed, and ate raw; and I have no doubt they did me much good. Once or twice, I was lucky in obtaining some turnip-tops, which I cooked, and enjoyed hugely. But there were thousands of hungry men on the lookout for these delicacies as well as myself, and therefore it took continued and persevering efforts for me to get a nibble once a week. This vegetable food checked the scurvy, and kept it at least within bounds.

The hospital was at last moved into one corner of the prison grounds. One day it was rumored that vegetable soup would that day be issued to the sick of the prison. A man who could crawl was not considered sick. A poor sick fellow near begged me to take his dish and draw some for him. This I undertook to do, and after waiting some hours I got the soup, and returned quickly to the sick man. He was sitting on the ground, his hands clasped, and his head upon his knees. I spoke to him, but he did not answer. I

touched his hand — raised it — it fell lifeless from my
grasp; he was dead — died while sitting, waiting for
food in this mournful position. It was quite common
for men to die thus suddenly. In my squad I was
knowing to several instances of men's drawing their
rations, and dying an hour or two afterwards. I took
the dead man's place in eating the soup, for however
sorry I was for him, I was too hungry to refrain from
relishing the food. That afternoon, with a full stomach, I felt like patronizing everybody.

About the last of September, we learned from our
guard that five or six thousand rebel prisoners had been
landed on one of the islands, in possession of our forces,
in Charleston harbor, to occupy a stockade built for
that purpose. This, perhaps, explained the reason why
we were not put down under fire ourselves.

I had often, when low in health, and restless under
the restraints of captivity, turned over in my mind the
probabilities of an escape. The rations of the prison
were steadily growing less in quantity, and the extreme
negligence or the purposed plans of the rebels kept us
frequently for twenty-four hours without food. Rest-
lessly seeking some mitigation of these sufferings, it
appeared to me possible that some dark night I might
crawl on my hands and knees through and beyond the
guard. There was great danger of being shot, but
there were other terrors in prison which would thus be
left behind. I made a copy of a map of Charleston
and vicinity, determined to try my luck the first dark,

rainy night, favorable to such an undertaking. My
plans were vague and general, the idea of getting to
the water, and obtaining something to float upon down
the harbor in the night, being uppermost; or, if I did
not get a boat or a log, to get into the city, and trust
to some of the German people for a suit of clothes or
concealment. At any rate my condition might be
bettered, and could scarcely be made worse.

Under the inspiration of these ideas, one rainy night
in September, making a confidant of no one, I crawled
beyond the guard. I could hear their measured tramp,
and one stood so near to me that I could hear him
breathe. Indeed, I thought myself perceived, when he
wheeled upon his heel and walked his post in another
direction, giving me a good opportunity to creep by.
I got to a safe distance from the sentinel, then rising to
my feet, ran towards the north part of the Fair Ground,
forced my way through the dense foliage which enclosed
it, when there burst upon my vision with lurid glare,
ahead and about me, a number of camp fires, around
which soldiers gathered. "Halt!" came the sharp
salutation, close on my left. I heeded not the command, but ran, steering midway between two fires.
"Halt!" "Halt!" simultaneously came the order from
right and left of me. Still I ran on. Bang! bang!
bang! rang the report of three or four rifles, aimed true
enough for me to hear the angry z-z-z-z-t of the bullets
as they whispered death around my ears. Close upon
me, right ahead again, came the order, "Halt!" I

halted, answering the summons, "Who goes there?" which rapidly followed the command, "Halt!" by replying, "A friend." "Yank, surrender!" laughingly called out the sentinel. I obeyed promptly, as I heard him bring his musket to a full cock, with an ominous click, and saw uncomfortably near me the gleaming of the polished musket. All this occurred in less time than I have taken to relate it. "What in dog-gond-ation was yer tryin' to do?" interrogated the Johnny. "Trying to pick up some warm quarters," I responded, as I walked to the fire and commenced warming myself. "Reckon yer found it durned warm, when the Charleston Guards commenced to blaze at yer, old hoss!" laughed my captor. I tried to show my contempt by saying, "O, that's nothing when one is used to it." "I reckon I'd er let daylight through yer, before yer got used to it, if yer hadn't stopped 'bout as yer did." I laughed at him, thinking it best to take things easy, while he called the officer of the guard. "Well, I'll be durned," said he, slapping my shoulder as a compliment, "if yer arn't right smart, for a Yank, any way." While waiting for the officer of the guard, one of the sentinels gave me a hard cracker, and my captor presented to me a generous slice of "sow-belly," which, I couldn't help thinking, was an ample reward for the risks I had run. The officer of the guard came up, and began to question me as to how I got beyond the sentinels of the prison grounds. "Bribed them," replied I, not caring what answer I made, so long as I did not

give him any information.   He looked at me from head
to foot, seriously, for a second, then, as if struck with
my picturesque costume of rags, smiled and chuckled,
as if intensely amused, and said, "They must have
tooken a mighty slim bribe."

I slept by the warm fire, under guard, that night,
and the next morning was sent to the workhouse, in
the city.   This building was of brick, built on three
sides of a square, with two towers, one of which, I
noticed, had been split down, by collision of solid shot or
shell, from top to bottom.   Under the arched ways of
the building, which led from the yard, were two rudely-
constructed ovens, used by the officers for cooking their
food.   In the building were the quarters of Federal
officers.   The windows were heavily grated.   In the
yard was a high lookout tower, from which could be
seen the jail-yard adjoining.   I staid here two days,
congratulating myself on my improved quarters, which,
in contrast with the Fair Ground, were very comfortable, though I was not allowed inside the building,
and I was only fearful of being sent back to the Race
Course.   While prying around in the archways of the
building, I found, in one corner of a dark doorway, a
bundle of documents which threw light upon the purpose for which the building had formerly been used,
and the manner in which slaves were committed for
punishment.   The following is a sample of a few in my
possession : —

"Master of the Workhouse: Receive Jerry, and put him in sol. con.   Rob. Rowand.

 Aug. 14, '56."

            "July 10, '58.

"Master of Workhouse: Receive the girl, Mary, give her (15) fifteen paddles, and return to me.

        Sam'l Watson."

"Master of the Workhouse: Give Hulda 5 paddles, put her in confinement 12 hours, and return to me.

 Jan. 20, '56.   J. Ricker."

On the morning of the third day, to my great disgust, I was sent to the Fair Ground, under guard. I kept pretty still about my adventure, being a little ashamed of not escaping after so many trials, and my comrades merely remarked that they hadn't seen me around for a day or two, and did not know but that I had had my "toes tied together." That day I hunted up Jesse L., who was formerly a comrade in the engineer corps, and re-formed a kind of partnership, which had been, for a time, suspended — to sleep under the same shred of a blanket, cook, hunt vermin together, and take turns watching each other's traps, while one was in quest of potato peelings or drawing rations. Jesse was a good-natured fellow, who was accustomed to say of himself that he could "scarcely draw breath on the rations he drew, and was running down so fast he couldn't run around." He was capable of laughing at any amount of misery, and baffled and held death at arms' length by ingenious devices; and his "devil-may-care" temperament, which nothing could daunt, and his irrepressible drollery, which would bubble up from the midst of misery, made him a desirable companion, to lighten the loads of despair which hung around us like a pall of midnight darkness.

Colonel Iverson had left the command of the camp, and we were miserably starved and neglected, having, often, the mockery of uncooked rations issued us, when there was not a chip or stick in the whole camp with which to cook. It was during one of these periods of extra starvation, when we had not had food for forty-eight hours, when the strongest men among us, through weakness, staggered and fell in endeavoring to walk, that a well-dressed officer from the city rode to the entrance, as it was termed, where rations were usually issued, and made to the prisoners there congregated, waiting in hopes of receiving rations, the proposition to go out and work. The following, as near as I can recollect, was the substance and manner of his proposition.

"We wish you to work down on the islands, under guard, as prisoners; it is work which any of you can do — which, as soldiers, you have been accustomed to. You won't have to take a musket: there are none compelled to go; but those, after what I have said here, who do volunteer to go, will be made to perform the work required of them, whether they like it or not. In return, we will give you rations of flour, meat, rum, and tobacco."

Ah, well do I remember that the very mention of fresh meat and flour was enough, almost, to craze me at that time. I remember how wishful and longing those poor fellows looked. Yet I had seen so much of their constancy under suffering, that I was not prepared to hear them clamor as they did to go out and work for food. It was a cruel temptation. The poor fellows had become childish, and knew not what they were doing. Said an old Belle Island prisoner, standing at my side, "Some one ought to speak to these men; they are crazy with hunger." Under an uncontrollable impulse, I clambered upon an empty rice cask, and commenced to speak. "Wait," said the officer, addressing me, "until I leave." After this he said, "All those who wish to avail themselves of the opportunity, may go and get their traps, and be ready about dark to leave the prison." He bowed to me, and saying, "You can now listen to your friend," withdrew a short distance out of camp, sitting on his horse, where he could hear what was said.

My theme had in it inspiration. I think I never did, nor ever shall, speak with such effect as then. I commenced by saying, "This rebel officer has honorably stated what he requires of you. You understand that he wishes you to dig rifle pits for our enemies, though he has not squarely said so. However honorable it may be for him to make this proposition to hungry, suffering men, it is treason for you to accept." I then spoke to them of their *homes*, of their friends, of the *cause*, and

14

the pride they would feel when, some day, they should again stand under the old flag, true men, not traitors. I closed by saying, "I, too, am starving: it is the work of our enemies. You can see written all over me 'Long imprisonment.' We are famishing, but let us show our enemies that we are not hirelings, but patriots; that we can die, but will not be dishonored. Is there one here, after suffering for so glorious a cause, that will band himself with traitors?" "No," "No," "No," "No," "Go on," "Go on," came the answers, like a pæan of victory, from the lips of starving men — truly a victory of truth over death.

It was said some went out that night, after dark. I did not see them, and can only wonder that the desire for life was not strong enough to prompt more to go. Many, who had clamored to go, when the officer first made the proposition to them, came up to me, and, with tears, thanked me — thanked me for keeping food from their lips at such a price. Poor, noble fellows! One of my company boys was among the number, and said, "It was the right kind of talk, Sarge;" and tears streamed down his shrunken cheeks as he said, "I suppose I shall die before I get out; but I had better, for I couldn't look mother or sis in the face after being a traitor." Poor, noble fellow! he did die not a week from that day, and, as his pale face rises unbidden to memory, I can scarce but reproach myself that words of mine prevented him from saving life at even such a price. "My heart rose up in my throat," said another, " at thought of the Stars and Stripes, and I wouldn't go for a brigadier-general's commission in the Home Guards."

Imagine me as an orator, clothed in picturesque rags. My wardrobe consisted of a pair of pants, remnants of a shirt, which hung in tatters from the neck-band, and an old torn hat, which looked like a letter A, rent by a dog. My pants were full of holes — so many mouths eloquent of misery. A decently-dressed, better-fed prisoner would not, perhaps, have affected my comrades by words so easily. It was because I was one of them, suffering with them, that they listened so earnestly and responded so eloquently. Their hearts were right, and needed only a monitor.

Sunday afternoons were holidays among the negroes of Charleston, and, dressed in their best " clo'es," they came to get a " peek " at the Yankees. They acted like overgrown children, and, when the Secesh artillerists pointed the guns towards them, as if to shoot, they ran screaming away.

During the last of September, two citizen prisoners of our number went down Charleston Harbor on the rebel flag-of-truce boat, expecting to be paroled or exchanged. One of them was paroled, and, as no arrangements could be made for the disposal of the other, he was brought back. In sight of the old flag and the friendly uniform, and then to be dragged again to an imprisonment which was to end — when or how no one knew — how great a disappointment ! The poor fellow pined away, lost courage, and soon died. Better for him had he never sailed down the harbor, with high hope of liberty, that pleasant morning.

About this time it was rumored that the yellow fever had made its appearance in camp and in the city. But there were so many rumors continually in circulation among us, that we knew not what credence to give them. October came, and we were told that a removal of the prisoners would at once be commenced. A number of cases of the yellow fever had occurred in town, and humanity, no less than the sanitary condition of the city, demanded our removal. I would have been willing to remain behind and take the risks, as, on the whole, our condition was liable to be worse at any other place than here.

A detachment of prisoners was sent away the first of October, and about two thousand every two days continued to be sent off, until the camp was cleared. On or about the seventh day, all the remaining squads of the prison, except the hospital department, were ordered to be ready to move on the morrow. About dark a pint of beans, a half pint of Indian meal, and a few spoonfuls of rice were issued to each man, for three days' rations. We got no wood to cook it with. That evening Jesse and myself cut into small pieces the sticks used to raise our blanket on, and, obtaining half of a canteen to cook in, commenced to prepare our rations. First, we boiled the beans, — of course without salt or pork; and, as we had no means of taking them with

us, and were hungry, ate them, for convenience and
to keep them safe from pilferers. Then we boiled
our rice, and, stirring up the Indian meal with it,
cooked a johnny-cake in our canteen. All around us,
gathered in anxious groups, were men engaged in similar occupations, and the casualties happening were
curiously ludicrous. Men were continually falling into
the shallow wells around them. It being the last night,
the prisoners used such fuel as they had liberally, and
indulged quite freely in pitch-pine torches. Every moment or two might be heard a " chug " and splash, which
proclaimed that some wandering star had fallen from
its orbit into a well. The position was more vexing
and comical than dangerous. I had been not a little
amused at seeing others precipitated into wells, and had
made up my mind that I would keep out of them. How
fallible are all resolves! While creeping on hands and
knees, and not thinking of the proximity of wells, I
was suddenly precipitated head foremost into one about
six feet deep. Jesse caught me in the act of scrambling
out, and, as I sat rubbing the sand out of my hair, and
trying to keep the water from running down my back,
he commenced to poke fun at me. "Ben in bathin',
old fellow? Better stand on yer head, and let it drain
off," said he, referring to the moisture, elevating his
torch, so as to get a better view, and stepping back,
chuckling. Suddenly, splash went something, and
Jesse was invisible : he had disappeared into the recesses
of the earth. It was then my turn to laugh. Thus

we made merry over our misery, which, ordinarily, would have dampened the fun of most people. Was it not as well to laugh as cry?

The morning dawned, and found our rations cooked into a mysterious, black-looking substance, which we called a johnny-cake. We fell into line when the order came, in a hurry to see what fate and the Johnnies would do with us next. We were speedily marched to the northern entrance of the Fair Ground, where, after going through with a good deal of the usual counting, we were packed on board of box cars, and went slowly on our way in a northerly direction.

As the cars were leaving Charleston we caught a glimpse of the Federal officers, who were embarked on board of box cars, *en route*, as I afterwards understood, for Columbia. Along on the railway, for quite a distance out of Charleston, were families of white people, living in box cars, having their beds, and kitchen furniture, and stoves therein. This I had noticed in all my transportations through Secessia. At Macon and other points it was quite as common as on the double and turn-out tracks near Charleston.

Our route from Charleston to Florence was unmarked by extraordinary occurrences. There were several men shot by the guard, while trying to escape by jumping from the cars while in motion. At every stopping-place those of our number who had died during transportation were left along the route for burial. A dickering trade was kept up along the way between the guard, who were stationed on the top of the cars, and the prisoners. At one place where we stopped to wood up, while the vigilance of the guard was relaxed, I slyly got off the cars and crept under the platform of the depot, and was much chagrined when one of the Johnnies came along and stirred me out of my hiding-place, with admonitions to "git into them thar cars."

CHAPTER XII.

IT was pitch dark and raining furiously when we
arrived at Florence, our destination. We were
marched into a field, and took up our quarters among
the hillocks, where had once been a cornfield. Water
and mud combined to make the ground an uncomfortable bed that night. During the night a large number
died. Willard Robinson, who had been complaining
some few days, died that night while lying under the
same blanket with his father. The morning dawned,
and the unhappy parent found his son lifeless by his side.

Smitten with grief, the father sat by the side of his dead boy, who had shared with him the perils of battle, and had been a companion in all the misfortunes and miseries of imprisonment. That father, who had more than once refused to purchase life by dishonor, would see that son no more. It was agonizing, but harder still the sequel. We went to the officer of the guard, and entreated for permission to bury the body. This poor boon for the father was refused. We then asked that the father might have the privilege of seeing him buried. This, too, was refused us. Their ears were deaf to the father's pleading — their eyes were blind to his tearful sorrow. The father spread the poor remnants of his handkerchief over the face of his dead son, folded his dear hands — it was all he could do. With a heart breaking with grief, he turned to leave him there, never to meet until the glory of a brighter morning should bring them together.* Not daring to look behind lest we should see rough hands stripping the dear body, we turned and commenced our march for the prison, — about a third of a mile distant.

At last a "stockade" similar to that of Andersonville loomed up before us. We were marched through the gates, which were closed upon us, to be opened, perhaps, never again during life. We were assigned to a portion of the stockade, and set ourselves at work to better our condition. The prison, like that of Andersonville,

---

* This was the last of several young boys who joined our company from the same New England village — South Scituate.

was situated on two hill-sides, with a branch of muddy
water running through the centre, embracing, in all,
about twenty acres.   To prevent tunnelling, on the
outside a ditch was dug, the dirt from which was
thrown against the stockade, forming a kind of walk
around the entire prison, which brought the top of the
stockade breast high to the sentinels, who constantly
walked their posts.   These sentinels did not seem to
have the fear of Jeff or the Confederacy before their
eyes, as, when at night the hourly cry went round, they
often closed their " — o'clock, and all is well," with a
poetical flourish of their own — "And old Jeff's gone
to h—l."   "What regiment do you belong to?" I inquired of one of them on the morning of my arrival.
"I belong to the fifth Georgia; Cheatham, he's our
adjutant."   I afterwards found out who Cheatham was
— a comical, jolly grayback as ever graced the Confederacy.

Four others, with myself, formed a mess, and commenced constructing a shelter.   For this purpose we
dug a hole in the hill-side, about three feet deep.   Two
sticks were then set into the ground, across which was
tied a third for a ridge-pole.   Over this was stretched
an army blanket.   The front and rear ends, of course,
were open, as we had nothing with which to stop them
up.   When it rained, we sometimes stopped up one
end with our garments.   In this grave-like place four
human beings lodged, kept their "traps," and called it
their home.   We found sufficient wood for cooking

purposes by peeling the bark from the stumps of trees, while those who had the implements cut and dug at the stumps for fuel. A week or two after my arrival, I obtained permission to go outside the prison under guard, and get material for completing our apology for a tent, and returned rejoicing with as much untrimmed pine brush as I could drag. We stripped off the pine pins, and put them in at the bottom of our shelter, making a very aristocratic bed, which few in prison enjoyed. We then patched up the rear of our "shebang" with pine limbs, which made altogether quite comfortable quarters, compared with what we had formerly enjoyed. But we needed all this, and more too, to make up for want of circulation and vitality in our scurvy-stricken bodies, and for the inclemency of a South Carolina winter, which, however sunny the South is said to be, was very cold. I never suffered more with cold than at this time. The days were usually quite warm, but, from sundown to ten o'clock in the morning, it was, to our poorly clad, emaciated bodies, bitterly cold. My clothes, which I have before described, were full of holes, and my feet were bare. The frost in the mornings was like snow on the ground, and often, through fear of freezing or being chilled to death, barefooted men walked up and down the prison all night, longing, through intense suffering, for morning to come. Often, in the dead hours of midnight, I walked the frosty ground, pierced with the sharp winds which mercilessly sought out every hole in my scanty wardrobe, and the next day took my revenge by sleeping in the sunshine to make up for lost sleep.

From the day of my arrival in camp, I commenced making use of hard wood ashes and water to clean and rinse my mouth, and soon had the satisfaction to know that it was counteracting the effects of scurvy. Our rations at this place were as scanty as at Charleston. Our divisions for the issue of rations were the same. In no place did prisoners suffer so intensely, and yet in no prison was the commanding officer so inclined to make us comfortable. Nothing, however, short of a complete change in their mode of living could now benefit the majority of prisoners. A large number of men, after a few weeks, were paroled to remain outside the prison during the day to cut wood for the use of the camp, while our police were urged by the colonel commanding into building log shelters for those of the sick who could not help themselves, and made to keep the prison quite clean and orderly.

As it was impossible to obtain water without going into the mud and water over knee before getting to the branch or brook which was the only supply of the prison, there were men who made a business of obtaining water for others, the common fee for so doing being a "chaw of tobacco." "Who wants a pail or canteen of water for a chaw of tobacco?" was as common a clamor as "Have a hack?" "Have a hack?" at our metropolitan railroad stations. Near the brook a hundred or more men would be gathered, who would feel repaid for half a day's waiting, wading, &c., with one or two diminutive chews of tobacco. Sometimes might be seen men around camp selling the proceeds of these labors for rations.

During the summer we had been annoyed with flies, mosquitos, fleas, and all such kindred plagues. As cold weather advanced, we got clear of these; but a greater annoyance set in, little dreamed of. The vermin, not troublesome in warm weather, now, as the cold set in, took the benefit of the warmth of our bodies, swarming from our blankets and the ground upon our persons. Night or day there was no peace with them; they would not be still. Scratching only pleased them; for, where the skin was once started, they went to work eating into the flesh. The results were frightful, loathsome sores. I have seen sick persons whose flesh was eaten almost to the bone. I cannot, however, say whether the vermin ate the flesh, or only produced the irritation followed by scratching, which may have caused the sores. However disgusting such details, it is necessary that I should record them in order that the general reader may understand our condition.

At Florence the police organization, as I have intimated, was again revived under Big Peter as "chief of police." Their offices consisted in seeing to the police duties of the camp, guarding against the perpetration of nuisances, constructing shelter, procuring fuel for those not able to help themselves, and the carrying out

of the dead.   Under these arrangements, the camp
became clean and orderly, wood was more regularly
divided and dealt out, and the dead cared for more
decently than before.   There can be no disputing
that they accomplished much good.   But even this
organization was perverted into a tool of the rebels
for detecting the work on tunnels, and punishing those
who dug them by thirty stripes upon the bare back
with a cat-o'-nine-tails.   "Big Pete" becoming prostrated with a fever, a gigantic, ignorant brute, with
neither the good sense, good humor, nor the disposition to deal justly, which were characteristic of Peter,
took his place as "chief of police," and under his
misrule cowardly acts were perpetrated upon prisoners.
Those who incurred the displeasure of the rebels, or
their tool, the "chief," were tied to a whipping-post,
and were mercilessly punished upon the bare back
with that classic instrument, a cat-o'-nine-tails.   Sergeant English, of a New York regiment, had once
been instrumental in bringing this big brute before
the prison tribunal at Andersonville for the murder
of one of his company or regimental boys.   On some
trivial excuse, the chief brought Sergeant English to
the whipping-post, and, before even a form of trial
was through with, and while yet his hands were pinioned behind him, struck him repeatedly in the face
with his clinched fist.   It was only through the
instrumentality of Lieutenant Barrett, of the prison,
that he got a trial, and, nothing being proved against

him, he was released. Sergeant English then said he
would have justice; and I only wonder that S. has
never since been brought to trial for his brutal outrages
against prisoners.

In November the cold became so intense, our rations
so inadequate for the maintenance of health, the prospects of an exchange before the close of the war so
vague, and the chances for life so uncertain, that the
strongest heart recoiled at thoughts of the future.
Broken in health and spirits, they cast despairingly
around them in search of some means by which to
escape from the impending doom which threatened
them. Terrible were those days and nights of torture
and death, from which there seemed no release. Most
of the prisoners whose hearts had been buoyed so long by
hope of exchange, parole, or deliverance by raids, now
sank in despondency. Taking advantage of this hopelessness among prisoners, a recruiting station for the
Confederate army was opened near the stockade, the
officers of which came into prison for recruits. There
were some among us so hopeless, so lost to every
feeling but hunger, that they bartered their honor for
food, and took the oath of allegiance to the detested
Confederacy. Let those who blame them consider that
these men had been suffering the torments of Andersonville, Belle Island, Salisbury, Charleston, and Millen,
for many dreary months, and now before them was a
hopeless winter, without clothes to cover their nakedness, food sufficient to preserve health, or blankets

to wrap themselves in at night. Some, considering an oath taken at such a time not binding, went out only to risk their lives in an escape. Jimmy, a boy about fifteen years of age, had no blanket or cooking utensils. He was continually obliged to beg for the use of them from some one more fortunate. In his destitution, he had to walk nights to keep from being chilled completely through, which, with men in prison, was usually followed by death. His life was crowded with inexpressible misery. For weeks brave Jimmy endured these miseries. He had refused at Charleston to go out and work; but at last the tempter prevailed: he went out, took the oath, had enough to eat for one week, and was shot, it was said, while trying to escape the next.

Many died rather than stain their lips with the dishonor of such an oath. D. P. Robinson, whom I have twice before mentioned, had it urged upon him thus to save his life. His answer was, "My boy is dead. I shall go with the boy." Simple words, yet heroic. "Death rather than dishonor" has been sublimely uttered by orators and novelists, but never was its import so heroically realized as in many instances like those daily occurring in prison. I was, however, sometimes grieved to see men in comparatively good health going out to take the oath, men who possessed a blanket or overcoat. N. L. and A. H., men of my battalion, were of this number, in spite of promises made to me a few moments before. When my back was turned they went out to the recruiting office. So great was the indignation of the prisoners at the conduct of such men, that the rebels had continually to protect them by a guard. The rebels had no respect for them, and distinguished them from the genuine graybacks by the significant term of "Galvanized Yanks." It was true that a few under terrible suffering, with death looking them in their faces, took the oath as the last hope of life. Yet I cannot but be amazed at the general constancy with which starving men repudiated such conduct while surrounded by suffering and death. There are but few instances recorded where men exposed to such temptations so resolutely acted, suffered, and died for the right.

The hero who gives his life for a cause, while shouts of comrades cheer his heart, thrilling with grand emotions, is looked upon with admiration. But he who suffers gradual starvation, temptation, and despair, for many, many weary months, and at last seals his devotion with death, is he not the truest hero? Many a one lies to-day in his prison grave, which bears no name or mark to tell how he died, or what he suffered, or how true he was to the cause for which he renounced home, happiness, and life; but a grateful nation will recognize and remember in coming time the devotion which has done so much to perpetuate and preserve national life and honor.

Lieutenant-Colonel Iverson was in command of the prison, and a lieutenant named Barrett had the super-

15

vision of its interior. He was a rough, green, conceited brute, who never spoke without blasphemy, and never gave a civil word, or did a kind deed for any prisoner — a man with as few of the elements of good in his nature as I ever knew. I have always wondered that a man like Iverson tolerated such a coarse brute. I cannot account for it unless I take as an explanation an expression which I once heard him utter : "Barrett is just rough enough to scare the Yankees, and make them stand round." It was a task Iverson was too kind-hearted to take upon himself. Iverson paroled eight hundred men to cut wood for the prison, and continually urged upon our police, to whom he gave extra rations, the building of shelter, &c., for the destitute. But this took time, and meanwhile hundreds were dying. It was not life, it was mere existence.

From the time I made my escape from Andersonville I was troubled with aching limbs, which, after my release, terminated in paralysis of my legs, and left side, from which, I have not as yet recovered sufficiently to walk without a crutch.

About the first of November came the joyful announcement that clothes had arrived from Charleston, sent by our Sanitary Commission. The excitement among the prisoners was very great, and a hundred at a time were marched to the prison entrance, to be inspected and supplied according to their merits of raggedness. But the supply was inadequate to make us anything like comfortable. Some poor creatures,

who for months had been without blanket or coat,
got one, robed themselves in it straightway, and
lay down, as if they had reached at last their ideal
of comfort. The police did much to distribute these
articles of clothing where they justly belonged. I
had no shirt. Some shreds simply, hanging from the
neck-band, proclaimed that my person had once rejoiced
in such an article. I had no shoes, and holes formed
the principal part of my breeches. All my ingenuity
could not make my wardrobe break joints to cover my
nakedness. Yet there were so many worse off than
myself that I was justly overlooked until the last.
When it became certain that no more urgent cases
were to be supplied, then I got a cotton shirt. This
I was lucky enough to swap for a red flannel one, in
the possession of which I was positively happy for a
time.

Somewhere near this period the south-west corner of
the stockade was separated from the main prison for a
hospital. Here rude barracks were built, and outsiders,
not regularly admitted, were kept out by a police force
detailed from the prison. Once I escaped their keen
eyes, and flanked into the hospital, where a friend gave
me such a stomachful of wheat bread and sweet potato
soup that its very remembrance gladdened me for
weeks. Thus slowly the clouds began to break, and
luck turned in my favor. There were men in prison
who bought four or five sweet potatoes of the rebel
sutler, and, cooking them, sold enough to buy again,

and get one for themselves. One morning I drew Indian meal for my ration, and traded it for a sweet potato. This was not so much in bulk as the half pint of meal, but the potato seemed to do me more good; and thereafter, when I could, I traded off my rations for sweet potatoes, under which diet, and my habit of daily bathing, if I did not gain strength, I managed to keep what little I had. Sergeant Charles Stone, of a Maine regiment, gave me at this time about a dozen potatoes. I shared them with comrades, and as the irrepressible Jess described it afterwards, "The way we walked into those potatoes" would have made the reader smile to behold.

At one time officers came into the prison, covertly buying greenbacks of the prisoners. As they went out of prison, Colonel Iverson caused them to be arrested, seized upon the greenbacks, and devoted the money so obtained to buying potatoes for the sick prisoners. I state these facts from a sense of justice towards a man who showed consideration for prisoners. Though Iverson did harsh things through his red-headed brute tool, Barrett, such as hanging men by the thumbs, &c., in the main he intended to deal justly by the prisoners, which had been unusual in my prison experience. He once stated to me that the men would get more food if he was not positively limited by the quantity and quality issued to him for that purpose. He could issue no more than he had.

Before the presidential election at the North, the rebels evinced intense interest in its result. They were anxious for McClellan's election over Lincoln, or, at least, for Lincoln's defeat. To test the sentiments of the prisoners, and thus form some estimate of the manner the States would go in the pending election, on the day of election two bags were placed on the inside of the stockade. Those who were in favor of Lincoln were to put a black bean into a bag, and those for McClellan were to vote white beans, which were provided for this purpose. We were marched by hundreds, and deposited our ballots. It was understood that if a majority of votes were cast for Little Mac, we should get extra rations that day. The result of the ballot was about fifteen hundred for McClellan and six thousand for Lincoln. There were about ten thousand men in the camp, but all did not vote. The rebels were disappointed at the result. When the vote was declared, the prisoners gathered at the place of election, cheering and singing patriotic songs, and Colonel Iverson forbade their being interrupted.

CHAPTER XIII.

Philosophy of Humor in Suffering. — Natural for Men to seek for
Sunlight. — Smiles and Tears. — Lightness of Heart. — Jesse L.
a Sample. — His comical Demeanor. — Jess as a Pair of Bellows.
— A queer Remark. — Dealing out Rations. — All Eyes on the
Meal-bag. — Squeezing the Haversack. — Eyes big with Hunger. —
Jesse's Tactics. — Raising the black Flag.— More Truth than Po-
etry.— Jack E. — Herbert Beckwith. — Jess cooking under Diffi-
culties. — Scurvy. — Combination of ' Disease, &c. — Torturing
Memories. — Character developed by Suffering.— Arthur H.
Smith. — A Break. — Death of Comrades. — A Political Creed. —
Escape by Bribery. — Coincidences. — Instances of them. — De-
cember, 1864. — A Call for Clerks. — Colonel Iverson's Surprise.

UNDER the circumstances described in the foregoing chapters, it may seem to the general reader
inconsistent with human nature that those so situated
should see and realize anything like the grotesque and
humorous in the kind of life which, as prisoners, we
endured.　This is true as applying to the many; but
gleams of wit and fun were all the more striking when
contrasted with the dark background of prison misery.
In reading these pages, it may sometimes appear to
critical readers, that the author has exhibited too great
a disposition to indulge in levity or humorous delinea-
tions, to satisfy them that he was, after all, so great a
sufferer, and that the horrors of prison life, as depicted,

were not overdrawn, or, at least, exceptional in their application. Human nature remains the same under all conditions, and, though modified by circumstances, must act itself out, strange though some of its phases may appear. Humanity is complex and curious as a study, especially when seen under extraordinary circumstances, where the conventional courtesies of etiquette, which mask the character of most men in the common conditions of society, are dropped, or cast aside unknowingly from its features.

There is a physical and mental disposition, common among most men, when their condition is overcast by the gloomy shadows of misery and want, to seek for and enjoy some ray of the sunshine to which they may have been accustomed, however little there may be. So, in our prison sufferings, if we could sometimes get glimpses of anything like, or even suggestive of, the sunlight of other and better circumstances, amid the gloom of our squalidness, we were inclined to enjoy and appreciate it, though the elements from which the gayety or humor would be produced, were often, perhaps, more properly causes of agonizing tears than of hilarity or glee. Lamentations and laughter, mingling together, as is frequently seen in children, were phenomena sometimes witnessed among the prisoners. In this manner the one element mitigated the keenness of mental and physical sufferings produced by the other, without which, often, the one, if not beyond endurance, would have proved much harder to bear. In this way Nature sometimes kindly tempers the winds of adverse circumstances to the shorn lambs of wretchedness. There are several causes contributing to produce this condition of mind, but first among them is the disposition to make the best of one's circumstances, practicalizing the old adage, "It is no use to cry for spilt milk."

All reflective minds seem intuitively to assume that nothing can be gained by taking gloomy views of unhappy circumstances, over which they have no control; that it is better to be merry than sad; better the laugh should well up from a sinking heart than to give expression to groans of despondency, for these outward expressions are oftentimes instrumental in producing a joyous or saddened condition of mind. To one whom Nature has gifted with much buoyancy or lightness of heart, who has, perhaps, a keen appreciation of the ridiculous, there are no circumstances where the combinations of the ludicrous are so often possible as in the midst of the most extreme misery. There seems, amid such scenes, to be but one step from the tragic to the laughable, and the transition is so readily and easily made from the one to the other, without change of scenery or character, that feelings of mirthfulness and lamentations not unfrequently mingle in the same utterances. This is, seemingly, typical of their relations, and symbolizing the narrow division which, once overstepped on either side, readily produces either of the two extremes. The squalid and ill-conditioned circumstances of the

peasantry of Ireland seem to have given them a love
for drollery and an appreciation of the humors, conceits,
and vagaries which will often spring up and group
themselves around great poverty.

There were usually two opposites of character continually mingling together in prison, one borrowing
gloom from the future, the other more hopeful, with
tendencies constantly uppermost to laugh at the ridiculous and comical, seen gleaming through the clouds
of despondent wretchedness. Blessed was he who retained this happy disposition; who, forgetful, for the
moment, of himself, could still find in his heart the
elements of mirth and humor. It increased his chances
of life, when others, of opposite mould of character, were
almost sure to die. Jesse L. whom I have more than
once alluded to in this narrative, was a fine sample of
this phase of character — a man whom no amount of
suffering from short rations and cold could dampen or ·
dismay. If he ever entertained serious thoughts, he
kept them to himself, or made them known in so droll
a manner as to make one laugh in spite of hunger and
other miseries. A certain comical grimness in his phys-
iognomy was heightened by a dirty face, where, perhaps, a few tears, shed over others' misfortunes, or a
smoky fire, had worked lines of queer and grotesque
import, which an artist's pencil rarely could have imi-
tated or excelled. On one momentous occasion, when
a dish of mush trembled in the balance and was found
wanting, for the need of fire to cook it, Jess desper-

ately turned himself into a pair of bellows, and, thus engaged, blew about all the strength and wind out of his half-starved body, until, at last, despairing of obtaining any flame, he looked up, coughed, and, with an inimitable grimace, said, "Look 'ere, Sarge; just help me — can't you?" Seeing how fruitless he had been in developments, I modestly disclaimed having any ability in the blowing line. "Well," said Jess, winking and coughing with smoke, "you might put one hand on my stomach and the other on my back, and squeeze a little more wind out of me at that smoke."

The dealing out of rations for a squad of twenty men was an interesting daily performance, spiced with hunger and an anxiety on the part of each to get as much if not more than his comrades. On such occasions, in my squad Jesse usually officiated with a spoon, dealing around, in regular order, one spoonful of meal and then another, until it was all given out. At times it of course overran more than even spoonfuls to the whole, sometimes half of us getting one more than the rest. This was equalized by commencing to deal out the rations where, on the day previous, they left off giving the extra spoonful. Each man had a number, by which, at ration time, he was known. During such a performance, the meal-bag, or haversack, was the focus of all the twenty eyes interested in its fair distribution. Dead silence reigned throughout the squad. More solemnity and anxiety could not have been infused into any other transaction of our life than was given to this matter, so near our hearts. Great interest was usually shown in having the bag, or haversack, in which was contained the meal, well shaken and scraped of its contents. One day the flour which was issued went but little over three heaping spoonfuls apiece, and hungry eyes were turned to that common centre, the meal-bag. Jesse turned the haversack, shook it, and scraped it with desperation, knitting his brow, then, looking grimly around on each silent, anxious face, with a twitch at the corners of his mouth, and in a snuffling tone said, "Boys, yer eyes won't have to be very big to be bigger than your bellies, if they feed us this 'ere fashion long."

At another time some hungry customers persisted in critically examining the bag (after Jess had got himself into a sweat in scraping it until not a speck remained which would have proved a temptation to a pismire), to see that it contained no more meal. Jess threw the bag towards them, remarking, "If yer can look any meal inter that 'ere bag, I wish you'd give a look inter my stomach!"

As winter advanced, in common with other prisoners, Jess experienced great trouble from those tormentors of our flesh, the vermin. Almost continually during the day he had his nether garment off, engaged in a war of extermination, when, as he expressed it, he raised the black flag, and gave "no quarters" to the enemy. Drury, a quizzical fellow of our acquaintance, came upon the busy Jess thus engaged, and remarked,

"Now, old feller, you seem to be at them about all your time." "Yes," said Jess, suspending operations for a while, to scratch his back, "it's a pooty even thing; me and these fellers take turns." "How so?" inquired D. "Why," quietly remarked Jess, with a droll snuffle, "I torment them all day, and they torment me all night!" "In that remark, O Jess, was condensed more vigorous truth than poetical *licence*," remarked D., as he walked away, leaving the undaunted Jess still "at um."

Damon, another comrade of mine, shared, in common with the rest of us, a very spare diet. One day, after being diligently engaged in compressing his pantaloons around him, in order to keep them on, for the want of suspenders for that essential purpose, with a long-drawn sigh, shook his head, and remarked, "There's one consolation: if I keep on growing slim in this way, there'll be cloth enough in this pair of breeches to make two pairs, which will give me a chance for winter." The idea was so amusing that laughter was irrepressible.

On another occasion I noticed my hungry comrade Beckwith eating a suspicious-looking substance, which bore a close resemblance to raw dough, rather than bread. "What, Beck., eating your flour raw?" I inquired, just to see what he would say. "Raw? Yes!" exclaimed he, with mingled tones of indignation and humor; "I shouldn't wonder if 'twas just the thing to stick to my ribs and make me fat." Thus it was that starving, suffering men, while battling for life, laughed at fate, and threw their jokes in the face of famine and wretchedness.

On first entering the Florence prison I saw Beckwith almost daily. He always met me with the same brave smile, and with a quick, merry sparkle of his fine blue eye. I remember his jocular expression used to be, when we met, "Hey, old boy! what der you think of this — don't you? Tall living, perhaps you believe." But there came a change: his steps grew more and more feeble; his blue eyes looked their merry smile no more. He lived to reach Annapolis, and died without the longed-for sight of loved friends and home, where and among whom he had hoped to lie down and be at rest. Brave comrade! poor fellow! farewell! No more shall loved ones gaze upon thy merry, soul-lit face; no more will ring thy light, full-hearted laugh.

How many faces, like his, pale with dreadful suffering, come up like ghosts in households throughout the land, bringing to anguished hearts wails of bitterness and sorrow, which nothing can heal in this life! How hard the task, among our northern homes, to forget or forgive those who committed the crimes which mercilessly starved and tortured helpless men and youth, sent from every village of the land! At Andersonville, Florence, Charleston, and Belle Isle, their bones are an attestation of a stain which no future can ever wash from the garments of the South.

I one day found Jack E. intently engaged in stretching the remnants of an old shirt across two mud walls, built up like a dog kennel, leaving a space between almost large enough to admit two persons when lying down.   Jack was whistling away, as though well satisfied with the manner in which things were progressing, when I remarked that I couldn't see the use of the old shirt, as it would neither keep out cold, wind, or rain. "Well," said Jack, stopping suddenly in his whistling, with a puzzled gaze fixed on his "shebang," then looking up, with a triumphant grin, "I don't suppose it will; but won't it strain some of the coarsest of it?"

During a rainy spell at Florence, at one time it became almost impossible to start a fire, and wood produced, at best, little besides smoke.   The persistent Jess, under these circumstances, was indefatigable in his efforts to choke down the smoke and blow up the fire.   Being defeated time after time, at last perseverance was rewarded.   The little fire blazed, and Jess's face glowed with eager satisfaction as he held extended over the coals a split canteen, containing a concoction of flour and water, which the poor fellow's stomach was sorely in need of.   He was at the height of satisfaction, when some clumsy fellow, in passing, stumbled and fell, putting out the fire, and sitting in the identical canteen, and on the contents of which poor Jess had centred his ambition and appetite.   With one blow the prospects of Jess for a supper and a fire had disappeared.   The strain on his nerves was too much; he burst into tears, and from tears to a discordant wail of chagrin, disappointment, and hunger.   But, seeing the destroyer of his hopes, Venus-like, rising from a small sea of paste, his sense of the ludicrous was awakened, and Jess, bursting from a howl of sorrow and dismay to laughter, exclaimed, "Old fellow, if you'll set over that fire till it bakes, I'll go halves with you."

It was often piteous to see men struggling with despondency, hunger, and cold, in an attempt to preserve life. Men whose half-clad bodies were chilled through were to be seen moving feebly around during the night, uttering agonizing wails and moans, in an attempt to keep up circulation, and retain life in their wasted bodies. I recollect some half a dozen naked forms, out of which the likeness of human beings had been starved, with chattering teeth, groping around in prison, without a shirt to their backs, their gaze idiotic, and their speech confused and incoherent. Staggering feebly, they fell and died by the brook-side and in the sloughs of the quagmire, or by the dead-line. All human language fails to depict these scenes, and their very remembrance chills my blood with horror.

No imagination can picture the wretchedness of the hospital at the camp. Not one half of its inmates had their senses; their bodies begrimed with dirt, their limbs swelled and discolored with scurvy, or covered with the filth of diarrhœa, they lay often on the bare ground, in the rain, without shelter or blanket to cover their nakedness. Could the scenes occurring in prison be depicted and understood by the North in all their horror, the spirit of revenge would, I fear, have been aroused, and have gone forth in a war of retaliation and extermination against the South. How hard, alas! it is to comprehend scenes of wretchedness which elsewhere have no known parallel in the history of suffering men.

I have never seen a description given of the effects upon the human system of a meagre diet of entirely one kind of food. At Florence no vegetable food was ever issued, or meat, with three exceptional cases, to any but the hospital inmates. Our rations had more variety than we obtained at Andersonville, usually consisting of wheat flour, hominy, rice, or Indian meal. Dr. Hamlin, in his learned dissertation on Andersonville, assumes that to the scarcity of food were entirely owing those aggravated forms of scurvy with which the prison was recking. This, no doubt, contributed in producing them, by weakening the system and giving less power to the body to throw off the influence of disease; but, in my opinion, it was the entire absence of vegetable food, together with want of variety, which caused such unusually dreadful cases of scurvy.

The tendency of scurvy to bring out old diseases, and to reproduce and render chronic any weakness to which the system had a previous tendency, is also, I think, but little understood, as one of its effects. I believe the diarrhœa in camp, which, in a majority of cases, produced death, was only one of the aggravations of this disease, seizing upon that portion of the physical system which was weakest. Scurvy in the mouth produced scurvy in the bowels, which was followed by a general disorder of those functions. Old diseases, which were supposed to be eradicated, were revived by its influences, such was its tendency to seize upon the weaknesses of the system. I have of these matters, it is true, no scientific knowledge; but, having been witness to its workings in thousands of cases, I merely make the statement as a result of my observations on the subject.

It was true that starvation and mental despondency blended with so many forms of physical horror as to make it difficult to trace the distinct action of any particular disease. At Florence, as at Andersonville, the combination of them all produced feeble-mindedness and often insanity, which never partook in their character of fierceness, but were rather characterized by timidity of demeanor and incoherence of speech, in which often were mingled piteous tones of entreaty, low and tremulous with weakness; sometimes gleams of intelligence lighting the stony eye, or thrilling the voice with a wail of hopeless despair. No pen can picture or language express it; only those who are familiar, to their sorrow, with these scenes, will recognize the full import of my meaning. I seldom recall, willingly, these pictures of wretchedness; but they are too indelibly impressed upon memory, by the fierce brand of suffering, to be forgotten. Those sad, wailing voices, those clutching, restless hands, those pinched, despairing or meaningless faces, — all unbidden come back to me, with the horror of reality. Perhaps it

16

might be better to let such memories slumber in their prison homes; but they seem to rise reproachfully, and bid me speak. I am almost glad that language fails to convey half my meaning, for the hearts of parents and kindred would freeze with terror could they but see those loved ones in all their hopeless wretchedness.

Revenge is not tolerated in the light of our high, ennobling civilization; but when I behold the South, stricken and suffering from fire, famine, and the sword, as one of the results of the awful civil contest just closed, I seem to see the hand of God's retribution seeking out and visiting her crimes with chastisement. If in coming times, as in the past, she shall sin against the moral ideas of the age, or if we, as then, become participants in her crime, so shall we reap, with her, the punishment of those crimes.

There was a phase of character developed by prison life which was neither joyous nor sad in its outward expression, seemingly a quiet bracing of every nerve, and the concentration of all the powers of mind and body against disease and death, in which men neither laughed, nor smiled, nor cried, nor could anything move them from their impervious calmness of demeanor. Not even an exciting rumor of exchange, or prospect of speedy deliverance, seemed to start them from their impenetrable placidity. Imbued with a quiet inflexibleness of purpose, — and that to *live*, — they calculated every chance of life in each moment of time, yet never seemed to feel disappointment or passion. Like a rock in mid-ocean, lashed by the storm, they stood unmoved by the passions and longings that swayed and actuated the great mass of tortured mortality. I recall to mind one of this mould of character.

A comrade informed me one morning that S. was dying. I visited him, and found him suffering great bodily pain; but not an expression of it disturbed the calmness of his face. It was simply in the vice-like compression of his lips, and the convulsion of his limbs, that could be detected his great suffering. His hands were poor and wasted, seeming to be, simply, a parched skin drawn over angular bones. "Do you think you will live through it?" I asked of him. "Yes, I know I shall live as long as any one who does not get more rations than I do."

I did not believe him at the time; but, in spite of my unbelief, he lived, and is living still. He had a philosophy of his own in economizing life. He did not allow any passion or excitement to use up his vitality. He had a system of exercise, and, seemingly, was engrossed with profound reflections on his condition, studying himself and his circumstances to solve the problem of how he could best prolong life. I once asked him if he got down-hearted at the prospects. His reply was an index to his character: "No — there'd be no use in that;" as if his inflexible will controlled even the action of his mind, in that one purpose of living. Men of this iron mould were rare. It is uncommon, indeed, as a phenomenon, to see one possessing such stoical determination, such steady, unfaltering nerves, while battling for a foothold on life.

Sergeant Arthur H. Smith was a man who had something of this composition. Always quiet, determined, and undemonstrative, he took the hardships of prison life with dogged grimness of purpose, — as if to extract all the life there was from the food to be had, and infuse it into bone and muscle, for purposes of endurance. It was this calm, ceaseless persistence and inflexible purpose which were requisite qualities for carrying men through the quicksands of death which surrounded us. When Smith first came to Florence, he was sent out to gather wood for the prison. The guards did not have their muskets loaded that day, and, had they been, they were nearly as liable to go off the wrong end as the right one. Noticing all these facts, Smith commenced to organize "for a break." Suddenly, to the surprise of the Johnnies, about half of their prisoners filed quietly in another direction, as if acting under orders ; and so I suppose they were — from Smith. By the time the grayback sentinels began to understand the Yankee trick, the prisoners mentioned had scattered in all directions through the woods, and were not attentive to the repeated invitation of their guardian graybacks to "halt, thar !" It must have shocked the Johnnies' ideas of propriety to see the Yanks scampering off with so little notice. Smith was out on the "rampage" two or three weeks, but was finally captured in the vicinity of Wilmington. He had found friends among the black men, evidence of which he carried on his person, in the shape of some increase of flesh, and in a full suit of coarse gray clothes, and a shirt, made, I should think, from an old carpet. He came into prison with the same stoical demeanor and persistence of purpose standing out in his face — that of living and enduring to get home; which, it is needless to say, he achieved. He was my companion from Annapolis to Massachusetts, and lives to-day, shattered in health, but not shaken in the resolution to live as long as possible.

Sergeant Attwood, another comrade, was a man of opposite tendencies, with something of changefulness in his moods and disposition. He was, perhaps, as noble-hearted and brave a fellow as ever stood at a gun. Elated or depressed easily by good news or the reverse, his was not the temperament to endure the horrors of prison life. He sank under it, and, I believe, died at last amid the despondency and gloom of the prison.

Baxter, of Company G, went the same way, though he got his parole, and was on his way North. Shattered in mind and body, he roused himself at the prospect of going home, made the effort, and died. I recollect asking him, at one time, what he thought of the southern chivalry. His answer had in it food for thought, which, though it may be indigestible in these lenient times, was the spirit evoked by the barbarous usage of prisoners. "I have made up my mind," said he, "to one creed, political and religious, to govern my conduct when I get out of prison." "What creed is that?" I inquired. "To hate what they love, and love what they hate. I shall be sure, then, to be on the right side." If the future is to be a repetition of the past, I think his creed a safe one for the guidance of the North. But let us charitably hope that, now the great moral cause of southern inhumanity is removed, wrong ideas may also be revolutionized and supplanted by new ones.

At Florence the difficulty of escaping was increased by a deep ditch, already described, encircling the entire prison. This made tunnelling difficult and unprofitable, as it carried the tunneller, at best, but just beyond the stockade, where getting from the ditch would, under ordinary circumstances, attract or draw the fire of the guard. Yet men got out, by bribing the sentinels, and making their escape, with assistance, over the stockade.

One lucky fellow, who was the possessor of a watch, with several others, made his escape in this manner, and succeeded in getting into the Federal lines. I afterwards met him at the North, accidentally, on the train from New York to Boston, and had from him the particulars of his adventures. He and his comrades fell in with others who were escaping, formed a party establishing him as a leader, travelled nights, and slept in the woods daytimes. When set upon by dogs, they killed an entire pack of them, resumed their journey, reached the chain of mountains in North Carolina, and travelled on the table-lands of these elevations. At two or three different times they met white men, and, knowing it impossible to trust them, — although they, in each case, protested that they were Union men, — the alternative lay before them of killing them, or disposing of them in some manner so as not to endanger their own safety. Therefore they bucked and gagged them securely, and left them in the woods to their fate. It was hard that no other course was left to them, but desperate men, who had endured prison suffering, were in no mood to temporize under such circumstances. I wish I remembered and could give this man's name, and the full details of his escape, as narrated to me. It deserves to be put on record. My meeting him, in the manner described, was one of those singular coincidences which are stranger than the inventions of fiction. Many such coincidences and meetings occurred in my prison life. I will instance a few.

Jesse L., whom I have mentioned in these pages, was an old comrade in the engineer corps, in which I first enlisted. From the time of my first capture I had not seen him until I met him at Andersonville. Two men whom I had known at Belle Island very intimately, I met again during my second imprisonment. One of them I saw for the first time when we embarked on the flag-of-truce boat at Charleston. I sat down in the only place I could find, looked around at the man next to me, and thought I detected something familiar in his face: thinking him one of my casual acquaintances at Florence, I accosted him, when, to my surprise, he claimed to be one of my old Belle Island associates. At one time, in Florence, a German met his brother, whom he had not seen since he left home in the old country, some five years before.

The month of December was cold and gloomy, its chilly winds wailing through those long, bitter nights, like a requiem for the dead. The frost-whitened ground, which lay like a shroud over the prison; the various dreadful forms of despair, insanity, disease, and death; the shivering, half-clad beings, wandering with plaintive moans and chattering teeth up and down the prison, impress me now with terror, as one of the darkest times of my prison life. I can never think of that time without thanking God, with a full heart, for deliverance. As it is darkest just before dawn of day, so there is a gloom of circumstances sometimes preceding the light of happier days.

The rebel adjutant came into camp one day, looking up clerks to work upon a register of the prisoners, a copy of which was to be sent to our government in return for a like compliment conferred by them. I wrote my name and detachment, and handed it to the officer of the guard. In the afternoon, an orderly came into prison, and inquired for me. I accompanied him to the colonel's quarters, which was a log house, in which were a fire-place and two or three pine tables. At one of these sat a youngish, rather under middle sized man, dressed in gray. He looked at me with surprise, and said, with something of pity in his voice, " My poor fellow, can you write?" I took up a pen, which lay upon the table, and wrote upon a slip of paper a simple sentence, signing my name, rank, &c. The colonel drew it towards him, looked it over a moment, and said pleasantly, "Very good; that will do. Go into the prison and get your traps, and I will set you at work." "I have no traps," said I. "No cooking dishes?" "No!" It appeared to strike him as very strange. "Well," said he, "I'll feed you well out here." "I cannot agree to do writing," said I, "except for the prison." He looked up as if angry, and said, abruptly, "What difference does it make to you?" I said nothing. "Well, well, your Yankecisms shall be respected," said he.

CHAPTER XIV.

A New Life. — Plenty of Food. — Better Clothes and Treatment as a Clerk. — Register of Dead made up for our Government. — Large Mortality for the Number of Prisoners. — Many recorded "Unknown." — New Supplies of Clothing. — Colonel Iverson affected. — Fears from Better Diet. — Symptoms of Paralysis. — A large Arrival of Letters. — Longings for Home revived. — Rebel Adjutant Cheatham. — Georgia Troops. — Yankees employed on the Register, for Want of Competent Rebels. — General Winder. — His Dislike of Favors to Prisoners. — Unfeeling Remarks by him. — All sent back to Prison but the Clerks. — Inhumanity to Prisoners under him attributed to the Rebel Government. — An attempted Palliation by Iverson that Rebel Prisoners were ill treated. — Low Estimate of Yankees by Iverson. — Humor of Adjutant Cheatham. — His Description of a South Carolina Drill. — New Prisoners. — Orders to prepare for Exchange. — A Joyful Day. — A Poor Comrade. — Sad Sights. — A little Strategy to get off. — A Surprise, and Imprisonment ended. — Left Florence for Charleston. — Awaiting the Subsiding of a Storm. — A Massachusetts Rebel. — Compassionate Woman. — Under the "Old Flag" again. — Arrival at Annapolis. — Once more at Home.

I SIGNED a parole of honor, agreeing not to go beyond prescribed limits without a pass. That night I got a glorious supper of fresh beef and white bread, of which, however, I did not dare to eat as much as I wished for fear of the consequences. I slept in the Adjutant's cabin before a fire, and certainly thought myself altogether a lucky fellow. The next morning Adjutant Cheatham, of the fifth Georgia, gave me from his wardrobe a shirt and pair of drawers, which I considered very clever in one who had so poor a supply himself. Said he, apologetically, "I did have quite a lot of clothes when I came here, but I gave them all away to the bloody Yanks who were running around in thar" (pointing to the prison) "like yourself." I sent my former wardrobe into the prison to one of my comrades, and thus disposed of my vermin, or most of them. Still I had no shoes, or any other articles of clothing, except the said drawers and shirt; but they were woollen and warm, and I tingled all over with pleasant sensations from having again a full stomach and warm clothes. I went at once to work making up a dead register. This register showed, when completed, that over seventeen hundred Federal soldiers, prisoners of war, had died in this prison since its establishment, the last of September, 1864. The prison had never numbered over fifteen thousand men, and a good portion of the time five thousand would have covered the number contained therein. Many of the dead were marked "Unknown." What a burden of sorrows, disappointed hopes, and miseries were embodied in that word! Their names, their history all unknown, uncared-for, they died. Some mother, wife, father, or sister mourns them, or vainly waits for their coming. Each sound of footsteps at the door may cause their hearts to throb with expectancy; but no more in life shall they behold those faces which once gladdened the household. "Sick and in prison," they lingered and died, unknown.

Another lot of goods came from the Sanitary Commission, *via* Charleston, for distribution among prisoners during the middle of October. A guard was placed over them, and a Federal officer, who by mistake had got into the prison, was taken out and paroled for the purpose of taking charge of and distributing the goods among prisoners. Boxes also came through for several prisoners. The instructions were, that all boxes were to be examined, to see that they contained nothing contraband. The Colonel commanding undertook the task. The first box opened had a little pocket Bible, and on the fly leaf was written the name of the prisoner, with the words, "From your mother." As if this incident had roused some tender recollections of his own home, the Colonel turned quickly away, saying, "Put on the cover again, and let the poor boy have his box just as his mother packed it." Of the Sanitary goods I got a good suit myself, and had a chance to send my drawers and shirt into the prison for friends. The Colonel and Adjutant were very jealous of any of the paroled men having communication with the other prisoners. I had now been out at work on the register over a week, getting enough to eat, if I had dared to eat it. I had to exercise continual vigilance in regard to eating, and nothing but the most absolute self-control enabled me to keep from eating too much. I had had experience of this kind before, when released from Belle

Island, which was of great value to me. As it was, I scarcely passed a day without intensely griping pains and vomiting. At this time, too, I began to have my first symptoms of paralysis, and often collapsed in a heap while walking along, by my legs giving way from under me.

During my second week on parole, two rebel mail agents came to Florence, with about thirty thousand letters for the different prisons of the Confederacy. As the prisoners had been shifted around so much since imprisonment, it was impossible to tell exactly where they were. I was set to work to help distribute these letters, and look up the names on the register. Often the persons would be found to be dead; whereupon Colonel Iverson instructed me to write to their friends, informing them of the fact. While thus at work, it had never occurred to me that there might be letters for myself, until I came upon two. These letters informed me that all my friends were well, and though they were rather old, they encouraged me, and relieved many anxieties. Certainly, thought I, if fortune favors in this manner, I shall get out of prison before the war is over. Receiving these letters revived passionate longings for home and friends, which had been crushed for months under the accumulating miseries and mere struggle for foothold upon life.

The office where I wrote and lodged was the quarters of Lieutenant-Colonel Iverson, which I have once described. Paper was a scarce commodity, and we were not expected to make a very generous use of it. Cheatham, the rebel Adjutant, had before the war been a cashier in a bank. He was very kind to his Yankee boys, as he termed us, and was quite an able business man. The Adjutant had taken most of the young boys from the prison, and put them in a camp by themselves, providing them with much better rations than the stockade got. In this manner, about one hundred boys, from twelve to fifteen years of age, were cared for. He had one or two fine-looking little fellows around the office, whom he made great pets of. The Adjutant was very droll and humorous sometimes, and was never so happy as when he could get Eddy Knapp and another Yankee boy at dancing, or singing negro and comic songs. He used gravely to tell the women down in the village that these boys were Yankee girls, and at one time so completely humbugged them into the belief, that, prompted by curiosity, these Secesh dames one day made a visit to the prison headquarters, and commenced quizzing the Adjutant about his supposed girls, when the Adjutant, who had instructed the boys what to say, had their hair parted in the middle, and introduced them at the headquarters. The women asked them, "Be you Yankee girls?" "Yes, ma'am," was the answer. "Where do you stop o' nights?" "O, right in here with the Adjutant." Whereupon each Secesh dame took her snuff stick, which she had sat chewing, from her mouth, and sat in blank amazement, and when the Adjutant was out, said among themselves,

"This Cheatum is a drefful man." These women afterwards wished to look over the stockade at the prisoners,
and were so lost to all Christian feeling and decency as to
say, as they saw the emaciated creatures of the prison,
"Good enough for them Yanks; they needn't have cum'd
down to fight we'uns." Cheatham was a humane fellow,
generous in his impulses, yet a rebel of the darkest dye,
for all that. "Gol ding it," he used to say, "the Yanks
have got a powerful spite 'gainst us, and we have got
everything 'gainst them, and the best way is to fight
until it's knocked out of each other."

I often had a chance of seeing the "five Georgia"
and other rebel regiments in line. Their dress was a
medley of all the dry goods of the Confederacy, and
their drill in the manual of arms embraced every description of infantry tactics, from Scott to Hardee.
Some of the rebel privates one day passed headquarters,
and said one to the other, "Good quarters, arn't they,
Jim?" "Yes," responded Jim, "and full of them
devilish Yanks." The Adjutant heard the remark, and
turned to me, and said, "You see how jealous our folks
are when we do any kindness for you Yankees." I
have no doubt that the Colonel and Adjutant had to put
up with many caustic remarks from rebel soldiers and
citizens, whenever it was known they showed mercy
or favor to the starving, dying thousands under their
charge. "To tell the truth," said Cheatham, "I wouldn't
have one of you Yanks to work on that register, but
my rebs have no tact for business. They can fight like

the devil, but don't take to reading or writing, or such things." This was a tacit acknowledgment of the superiority of the Yankees in point of intelligence. It was full as rare to see a Yankee private who could not write, as it was to see a rebel who could.

While distributing the mail, of which I have spoken, the rebel general, Winder, made his appearance at the prison. He was a man apparently about sixty years of age, dressed in homespun Secesh citizen clothes, butternut-coat and gray pants, tall, spare, and straight in figure, with an austere expression of face, a firm, set mouth, a large Roman nose, like a parrot's beak, and a cold, stony, stern eye. I overheard a conversation, which took place on the morning of his arrival, between him and Colonel Iverson, who stood just under the cabin window, near where I was writing. Said Winder, in sharp, abrupt tones, "Colonel Iverson, I can't have all these Yankees running around outside the prison. What are they doing?" The Colonel explained that it was necessary, in order to provide the prison with wood, and to erect shelter for the sick. "No necessity," said Winder, abruptly; to which Iverson responded in a tone of remonstrance and entreaty, "General, the prisoners, in spite of all I have done, or can do, are starving." "Let them starve then!" said Winder, in sharp, angry tones, putting a stop to further conversation. In about an hour afterwards, Iverson came in with a pale, anxious, troubled look upon his handsome features, and walking nervously back and forth in the office, gave the Adjutant instructions to write the order sending back all paroled men except those at work in the office, and a few others, to the prison.

I mention this incident, as I think it furnishes the key to the general inhumanity with which prisoners were uniformly treated in all the rebel prisons. First, public sentiment South forbade to prisoners civilized usage; second, the inflexible Winder was in general command of all the Confederate prisons, and received orders direct from the chief actors in the rebellion. Winder afterwards died of disease contracted at Florence military prison, and thus poetical justice was dealt out. Mr. Christian, the rebel mail agent, related to me an instance of General Winder's severity and moroseness of temper. "In some battle around Richmond, a Brigadier-General was captured with other prisoners. Winder stood giving orders for the disposal of the prisoners. The Brigadier-General, in fawning tones, said, "Ah, General, what are you going to do with me?" Winder turned abruptly on his heels, replying in his sharpest tones, "Hang you, sir."

Several times I had conversations with Iverson and the Adjutant in relation to the treatment of prisoners, and in regard to slavery, in which my natural hastiness often got the better of my caution, and I expressed myself pretty freely. The Colonel defended the use of a dead-line, saying it was copied from our prison regulations, and very gravely stated that the Federal treatment of

17

rebel prisoners was as bad as theirs. "The treatment," said he, "on both sides is cruel." He instanced the treatment of prisoners at Fort Delaware, and said some of the boys of his regiment had been there, and that they did not get enough to eat, though he admitted it was through the rascality of the officers in charge of the distribution of rations. "They had tents," said I. "Yes," said he, angrily, "but we don't have any for our own men," and closed the conversation by going out. Some of my comrades, engaged in writing on the register with me, said, "Sarge, the Colonel has got his mad up, and you'll be sent into the stockade." Iverson stood only just outside, overheard the remark, and coming in at the door, indirectly reproved the speaker, by coldly saying, "I never think less of a man who has convictions which are not changed by his circumstances. I can trust such men." There were no men among the prisoners whom the Colonel had such contempt for as the "Galvanized Yanks." He treated men with severity when they intimated that they wished to "take the oath." He would say roughly to them, "You are traitors on one side — you will turn traitors to us the first chance you get; I can't endure a man who does not fight from principle." To Union men, who belonged to southern states, he was very vindictive and harsh, often calling them d—d traitors, asking them sometimes what they were fighting against their country for?

The Colonel's estimate of Yankee integrity and

intellect was a very low one. He was very much
prejudiced against them, and refused to see that the
general physical and mental condition of the prisoners
was owing to long suffering. He would sometimes
say in my hearing, of some poor creature who had
had all his humanity starved out of him, "Now, look
at him; he don't know so much as one of our niggers."
I once overheard a conversation between him and a
citizen. "These Yanks," said he, pointing to a squad
of prisoners, "are just like our niggers; you can't trust
most of them out of sight." Noticing that I heard
him, with true gentlemanly instinct, he stopped in his
remarks. When I got a little ahead of him in any
remark, he would say, "Sergeant, you are the doggondest stubborn Yank I have got," or, "You are a
heavy dog," and then closed the conversation by walking off.

Adjutant Cheatham used to delight in telling humorous incidents, and would even mimic his favorite rebels
in all their grotesqueness. Unlike most rebels, he was
free from the negro accent or patois, but would assume
it with great drollery when he was mimicking the
"South Caroleneans." I will not vouch for the truth
of the following incident, which he used to relate in a
manner which would have made a mule laugh. "I
was out the other morning," said he, "and saw a guard
drill that knocked all my ideas of that performance.
Groups of men were standing around their huge fires —
the mornings were quite cold — when one of the

South Carolinian officers came up, and pushing away a big fat fellow who had tied a tarred rope into his belt to make it reach round him, said, 'Eph, git from afore me, for I'm a-cold,' and proceeded to warm his rear by elevating his coat tail on his hands. Then looking around upon the group, he said, 'Now, boys, git into two ranks like tater ridges, for I'se a goin tu fling yer into fours.' After getting them into two ranks, he gave the order to 'right dress;' but the line didn't suit him. Eph, especially, gave him trouble. 'Eph, Eph, stick yer stomach in thar.' This Eph endeavored to do; but when his feet were in line his stomach protruded way beyond, and when his stomach was in line his feet were in the rear rank. Getting vexed at this, he pulled out his sword, and drew a crooked mark in front of the company, saying, 'Gol ding it, if yer can't right dress, come up ter that scratch.' They did this very satisfactorily, when he commenced to drill them. The first order was, 'Two ranks inter four ranks, double smart, right quick, git!' But in this manœuvre they got mixed up so bad that it wasn't tried again. He then commenced to drill them in the manual of arms. The person addressed as Eph seemed to take unkindly to this military drill, and his Captain addressed him in pathetic tones of remonstrance: 'Eph! Eph! I've told yer four times to bring that gun ter a tote, and yer hain't done it. Eph, yer have acted the plum fool!' Addressing the Sergeant of the relief, he said, 'Put this 'er Eph on guard near the swamp, where Cheatum won't see him.' And," said Cheatham, "without seeing me, away went the relief at route step, with arms in all positions but the right ones."

During the second week out on parole, about thirty men belonging to one of our merchantmen, captured just off New York harbor by a rebel cruiser, were brought into the prison. Iverson paroled the officers, but turned the common sailors into the prison to take their luck with the prisoners. The officers, who had enough to eat and good clothes, thought outside life about the hardest of anything they ever heard of, and were much surprised when I told them I thought they ought not to grumble, when men inside the stockade were starving. Two officers, Lieutenant Luke and Lieutenant J. Laughlin, were captured while trying to escape from Columbia, and brought into Florence prison about this time. Lieutenant Laughlin was captured in the same battle with myself, and as I was personally acquainted with him, I slyly gave him clothes, and went to the Colonel, at risk of being sent into the stockade again, and interceded for good quarters and food for them, which were given.

The last of November, orders came from General Hardee to commence making out parole rolls for the sick and wounded prisoners at Florence, who were to be sent to Charleston, at the rate of two thousand every other day. I, with others, went to work upon these paroles. What a joyful day it was to those men as at last they realized that they were going home, and with trembling, eager hands they signed their parole of freedom! I was at work making out these parole rolls, when a poor creature came with tottering steps to the table, and tried to sign his name. "You'll have to write my name," said he; "I'm not the man I was when you and I were captured at Plymouth." I looked up and recognized in this shattered wreck of humanity a Sergeant who belonged to Company G, second Massachusetts heavy artillery. I left my writing to another clerk, while I helped the poor fellow to my log hut, and gave him warm drink and food, and my blanket to lie on. The poor fellow tried to thank me, but broke down, crying like a child. He was not very coherent in his speech. He could only say repeatedly, "Do you think we're going home?" I assured him of the fact, and left him to resume my duties. Afterwards, when I returned, he was gone. He must have died on the way to Charleston, as I could never ascertain that he reached his home.

Day after day I wrote on the parole rolls, trying to see my way clear to get away with the sick and wounded. Men were hourly dying before headquarters. Mr. Christian, the rebel mail agent, repeatedly said, as he saw the poor fellows come out, feebly trying to cheer, that it was the saddest sight he ever beheld. I was instrumental in getting several of my comrades out of prison on the parole list, and finally summoned courage to make application in my own behalf, when I was told to be contented or go back to the stockade.

After quite a delay in transportation, an order came from General Hardee, to have fifteen hundred prisoners ready for transportation on the afternoon of the next day. The names were placed on rolls, giving rank, regiment, and company, after which the prisoners signed their names, or made their marks. These rolls were in triplicate, and each roll contained, I believe, about three hundred names. Like our army rolls, no erasures were allowed. When the order came I asked the Adjutant if I could put my name down on the rolls. He turned away, muttering something, and I proceeded to put my name down among the paroled. I then made out triplicates for the rolls, containing about three hundred names each, and anxiously awaited results. An officer commenced calling the rolls, each man stepping out into line as the names were called. The decisive moment at length arrived. My name was called. I laid down my pen, took my hat and stood in line. "Here! here!" exclaimed both the Adjutant and Colonel, in chorus, "what does this mean?" "I thought you told me," said I, with feigned surprise, "that I could go home with this squad, Adjutant." The Adjutant laughed, the Colonel looked pleasant, and I took courage. "Well," said Colonel Iverson, after a pause, "you can go; but you must confess that it is a d—d Yankee trick." When at last I left, on my way to the cars, the Adjutant said, "I'm glad for you; I intended you to go soon. I expect next you will be telling the Yankees what a d—d rascal Adjutant Cheatham was." And here I am telling all about him.

I left Florence that night. We were stowed on top and inside box cars. We travelled all next day, and arrived in Charleston about twelve o'clock next night. It blew hard, and was bitterly cold, when we were ordered off the cars, and had rations of hard-tack given out to us. Prisoners here and there lay dead and dying. It seemed too sad, when so near the promised land, that they should die. It was very cold the next morning, when we were on our march to the flag-of-truce boat; but what did we care for that? Were we not going home once more to see friends, and the dear old flag we had so often fought under, and which, God willing, we would fight under again? The wind was too heavy for the flag-of-truce boat to go, and reluctantly we were obliged to leave her; and from thence we were marched to Roper Hospital. From here, however, we were sent to the workhouse yard, which I have described in preceding pages. For two days we waited here, losing courage. Many lost hope, and many lay dead and dying around us.

The rebel commissary came in the evening to the workhouse yard. I inquired of him when we should be sent to our transports. His answer was encouraging; and in course of conversation he asked me where I belonged. I answered, "Massachusetts." "So do I," said he, extending his hand; "I belong to

Massachusetts." I inquired what part. "Marion," was the reply. I was acquainted there, and soon found I knew several of his friends. He took me and several friends out with him, and gave us quarters in Roper Hospital, which were very good. While at this hospital I came upon some letters. One of them was addressed to the board of physicians in charge, asking what disposal was to be made of the hospital if the city fell into Federal hands. This letter was dated just at the time of our first attack on Charleston, and shows that the rebels were not so confident at that time of withstanding the assault as they afterwards were.

We had been in Charleston three days, anxiously waiting, when the fog, which had been very dense, cleared away, and orders for our removal, together with ambulances, came to the hospital to move the sick to the flag-of-truce boat. Those not able to walk were brought out and laid on the sidewalk, where some of the poor fellows died. Peter Jones, one of my company, died thus. "It is hard," said he, sorrowfully. They were the last words he uttered.

While these men lay gasping on the sidewalk, a woman came to the red-headed surgeon, who superintended their removal, and asked permission to give the poor sick fellows some soup she had for them. He rebuked her severely, saying, "If you have any such thing to give away, give it to our boys, down on the Island. You show," said he, "what side you are on." Her reply was, "Anything for humanity's sake, doctor;

let me give these poor men something to eat." While she was thus occupying the attention of this Confederate ogre, she had sent some children around on the flank, who provided the sick with soup and gruel. The surgeon raved when he found himself outflanked and outwitted by a woman.

About three o'clock that afternoon, we were again on the wharf, near the flag-of-truce boat. What a joyful moment! yet it seemed too good to be true. We, who had been so used to being deceived, were incredulous to the last moment. As we stood on the wharf, the commissary whom I have mentioned came up to me, and, shaking hands, said in a tremulous undertone, "I'd give anything to be in your place, going to Massachusetts." Dear, proud old Massachusetts! thy children can never, wherever their footsteps wander, forget thee! At last we sailed down the harbor — were in sight of our dear old flag — at last were lashed to our receiving ship, were on board, and, thank God for his mercy, were again under the old flag. How our tear-dimmed eyes gazed at its folds, and we, with solemn, sobbing voices, said, "Thank God! thank God!" The link that bound us to the terrible past was broken; the gaunt forms, the famine-stricken faces of those who survived, and the torturing memories they will ever have of those dark days of death and despair, attest how cruel and merciless were those who had charge of rebel prisons.

I arrived at Annapolis on the 16th of December,

1864, and was soon at home among friends, where, upon my arrival, I was attacked with typhus fever, and the only sight I could bear upon the walls of my sick room during my delirium, was that emblem of our country's honor and glory, the Stars and Stripes. To-day, though broken in health, and perhaps crippled for life, I record these sufferings as a remembrance to coming generations, and dedicate these pages to the memory of the living and the dead, who in the "great struggle" have suffered or died in prisons, and upon well-fought battle-fields, for our country's preservation and honor.

APPENDIX.

"We, the undersigned, having been informed that Mr. Warren Lee Goss has written a book narrating his experience and observations in rebel prisons during the late civil war, which work may contain statements not readily accepted by some persons as true, desire unhesitatingly to testify that, from long personal acquaintance, we know him to be a gentleman of undoubted veracity and unquestionable integrity.

I. W. RICHARDSON, 68 Cornhill, Boston, Attorney at Law.

I. N. RICHARDSON, " " "

R. I. ATTWILL, Boston Daily Commercial.

C. B. WOOD, Town Clerk and Treasurer of Middleboro'.

S. B. PRATT, Editor and Proprietor Middleboro' Gazette.

W. H. WOOD, Judge of Probate Plymouth County.

L. A. ABBOTT, Pastor of Baptist Church, Middleboro'.

S. B. PHINNEY, Editor and Proprietor Barnstable Patriot and Collector of Port of Barnstable."

The following is from surviving comrades : —

"We, the undersigned, prisoners at Andersonville and other rebel prisons with Warren Lee Goss in 1864, take pleasure in bearing testimony to his unimpeachable truthfulness as a man, and to his honor and bravery as a soldier. In hours of sorest trial in those dreadful prisons (the horrors of which have been but one half told), when all finer sensibilities were pinched out of most of the men by hunger, sickness, and dread, he was ever a kind, patient, and faithful friend. Though suffering himself the common lot of hunger, exposure, and torture, he ever found time to comfort the sick and soothe the dying. When others sank, their hearts appalled by the prospects before and around them, his unfaltering courage upheld and cheered them. We are sincerely gratified at this opportunity of expressing our appreciation of his merits, and are pleased that so worthy a comrade and so kind a friend has taken upon himself the task of giving to the world an account of those days of suffering, despair, and death, when the strongest hearts were appalled with terror, and found hope and refuge only with God.

Residence.

S. J. EVANS, Sergt. Co. H., 2d Mass. H. A., Providence, R. I.

G. T. WHITCOMB,   "   "   N. Bridgewater, Mass.

S. F. SULLIVAN,   "   "   Lynn,   "

S. T. MEARA,   "   "   Salem,   "

J. W. DAMON,   "   "   Boston,   "

W. S. OAKMAN,   "   "   Charlestown, "

J. T. McGINNIS, 1st Sergt. Co. C., 5th U. S. Vols., Boston."

" The following is from the descriptive rolls of Warren Lee Goss, Acting Sergeant-Major Battalion, Second Massachusetts Heavy Artillery, on file at Washington : —

" ' Warren Lee Goss was a prisoner at Andersonville, Georgia, Charleston and Florence, South Carolina, and other rebel prisons. During the action at Plymouth (where captured) he behaved with great bravery.'

 (Signed)   " O. M. FISH, 1st Lieut. Co. H.,
    2d Mass. H. A., Commanding Company."

In the city of Washington at the time of the Wirz trial, there being survivors of Andersonville Prison present from all parts of the country, an organization was formed called the "Andersonville Survivors' Association." The following letter is from the President of that body : —

" I am glad some one has at last undertaken the task of writing an account of life in rebel prisons. I am sure you are acquainted (to your sorrow) with all the minutiæ of the subject. I am especially gratified that an old comrade, whom I have always found of unflinching integrity in all the trials of a soldier's life, — one who enjoyed the confidence of his officers, and esteem and love of comrades, — should assume a task like this. All returned soldiers who were acquainted with you testify to your kindness, bravery, and faithful friendship in those scenes of horror which were the accompaniments of prison life.

      " PATRICK BRADLY,
   " President Andersonville Survivors' Association.

" MILFORD, December 17, 1866."

The physician who attended the author after his arrival from prison, testifies to his physical condition as follows : —

"Immediately after the arrival of Warren Lee Goss from rebel prisons, I was called to see him professionally, and found him completely prostrated, suffering from scurvy, chronic diarrhœa, and cerebrous typhus fever, all of which were, beyond doubt, the effects of privations and inhuman treatment while incarcerated in those loathsome prisons; as also paralysis of the limbs, from which he has not as yet recovered.

"WILLIAM P. CROSS, M. D.
"BOSTON, December 18, 1866."

"I have had an acquaintance for several years with Mr. Warren Lee Goss, and cheerfully testify that I know him to be a gentleman of sterling integrity and worth. During the war he has performed good and patriotic services for the country.

"Last winter he delivered in this county lectures of unusual interest, giving details of his experience in the army, for which he received the thanks of our people.

"S. B. PHINNEY,
"Editor and Proprietor Barnstable Patriot.
"BARNSTABLE, December 1, 1866."

Colonel Archibald Bogle, Thirty-fifth United States Colored Troops, sends the publishers the following : —

"MELROSE, December 27, 1866."

" Messrs. LEE AND SHEPARD,

"Publishers, Boston.

"Gentlemen, — I have read over one hundred of the proof pages of a book written by Warren Lee Goss, Esq., entitled 'The Soldier's Story of Captivity.' I have peculiar pleasure in saying I formed an acquaintance with the author at Andersonville in 1864. I am but too familiar with many of the scenes which he depicts, and unhesitatingly testify that, so far as I have read, his descriptions of scenes of prison life are written with rare fidelity to truth, without exaggeration, and with a candor and straightforwardness which I am sure cannot fail to meet the warm appreciation of those who survived the terrors of that prison, and claim the highest consideration of every reader. As such I commend it.

"I am, gentlemen,

"Very respectfully,

"ARCHIBALD BOGLE."